Corporate Climbing

Making it in corporate America can fulfill your wishes, or crush your dreams, but be careful what you wish for – as the results can be monstrous…

Kevin Delano Hughes

DEDICATION

"For My Late Mother – Who Always Taught Me To Dream Big, and My Wife and Sons – Who Continuously Inspire Me. – Love You All."

"Wealth. Status. Happiness. A perfect life. All built on an ephemeral foundation, an impossibility masking a lie that if exposed, if openly acknowledged, would bring it all crashing down around our heads."
Sean Gibson, The Camelot Shadow

Table of Contents

DEDICATION iii

FOREWORD vii

PROLOGUE 9

CHAPTER 1   THE AWAKENING 15

CHAPTER 2   BROTHERS... 23

CHAPTER 3   BOLD ADVERTISING 30

CHAPTER 4   VOODOO MAN.. 39

CHAPTER 5   MISS ELLA 49

CHAPTER 6   WHAT YOU CAN'T UNSEE 54

CHAPTER 7   THE PROMOTION 58

CHAPTER 8   THINGS GO SOUTH 64

CHAPTER 9   THE PLAN 89

CHAPTER 10 THE WISH BOX 97

CHAPTER 11 UNICORN UNVEILED............................ 107

CHAPTER 12 DREAMING 124

CHAPTER 13 MOVING ON UP 129

CHAPTER 14 THE INVESTIGATION 151

CHAPTER 15 DOUBLE HOMICIDE 171

CHAPTER 16 ENOUGH 177

CHAPTER 17 THE UNDERWORLD 197

CHAPTER 18 RE-GIFTING.. 201

EPILOGUE.. 227

ABOUT THE AUTHOR... 230

FOREWORD

Achieving The American Dream is built upon capitalism and deeply rooted in a never-ending pursuit of materialism, where attaining excess defines success. Therefore, the more one acquires, the more successful one is viewed to be, which can contribute to an environment mired in greed. To advance within the higher strata of corporate America, many first pursue advanced degrees from institutions of higher learning, aiming to obtain impressive careers and lofty wealth goals. Some even delay the pursuit of relationships, marriage, and children, all to satisfy a hunger to make it within the corporate environment and acquire the heady trappings of wealth.

Corporate Climbing looks at the corporate environment as the vehicle and ecosystem for achieving the American Dream. The story encompasses *wishes*, *dreams*, and *gifts* and is set against a rabid backdrop of excess and murder. It features a protagonist and antagonist who represent the good and evil, respectively, that can exist and flourish within a corporate environment. At its core, the story revolves around the taboo topic of workplace bullying, unveiling a glimpse into man's inhumanity to man, revealed in situations that unmask the various personalities and pecking order within this hostile work environment. Adding the occult as a plausible solution and escape from the ills of the environment and an avenue to excel and prosper is introduced as an accelerant to this toxic mix and reveals parallels to the underworld.

Corporate Climbing is about average, everyday, working-class people trying to get ahead and railing against a system that is often difficult for immigrants and women to navigate and succeed in. The story challenges the reader to examine personal values and beliefs and dig deeper into what they want out of life and, more importantly, what they would be willing to do for it. For many, the story will serve as a cautionary tale that sometimes, even when we finally achieve all the materialism we desire, the essential moral and life lesson is that often we find that – *"All That Glitters Is Not Gold."* Corporate Climbing lies at the intersection of Money, Power, Sex, Greed, and Dark Magic. – Kevin Delano Hughes

PROLOGUE

The October sky is overcast and dismal. The heavens have a gray, ominous look, accompanied by a steady stream of unrelenting sheets of rain. It is a cold winter evening in Brooklyn, New York. The trees adorning the neighborhood streets strategically planted decades ago in front of every house on the block have long since lost their leaves, giving the tall oaks a stark and eerie appearance.

Michael has been looking forward to this day for weeks. So, although the weather is not cooperating, it is a day to be celebrated. Today is the surprise seventy-seventh birthday party for his father, John. Michael and his mother, Ruth, have worked extremely hard to plan this event.

The party is in the basement-level studio apartment of the Hill family's modest two-story brownstone house. The guests, which consist of close family and friends, have packed the tiny studio apartment. Everyone is busy socializing, enjoying food and drink, and awaiting the arrival of the guest of honor. Ruth and John Hill are getting dressed and ready upstairs, and the plan is for Ruth to lead her husband, John, downstairs at 7:30 p.m. sharp, and then all the guests will jump out and surprise John.

Michael walks around the room, making small talk with the guests. He spots his aunt Mary holding a glass of red wine and laughing with his cousin Anthony. He smiles at them and keeps mingling. As the Hill family are proud Caribbean immigrants, the food, and drink at the festive party are Caribbean staples and favorites, including peas and rice, curry chicken, oxtails, fish and fungi, and plantains. The aroma of the delicious cuisine wafts generously throughout the entire apartment. For drinks, there is cold mauby and fruit punch, along with beer, wine, and rum for the hard drinkers. There are freshly baked guava, pineapple, and coconut tarts for dessert. They even have a special treat for the guests in the form of grafted mangoes, which Aunt Mary obtained from the local Korean supermarket, even though they are out of season for this time of year. The mood is truly festive, and someone finds and turns on an old boom box CD player in the corner of the room, and soon The Mighty Sparrow's classic song, "Gene & Dinah," engulfs the room in pulsating calypso music, transporting everyone back to good party times and memories of the Caribbean.

Michael looks at his watch and sees that it is already 7 p.m. He smiles as he can't wait to see the look on his father's face when he walks in and sees everyone there.

The guests are having so much fun that they fail to see the ambulance's flashing lights as it quickly pulls up in front of the house, and the two paramedics jump out, frantically running towards the house with a stretcher and equipment.

It is now 7:30 p.m, and Michael looks at his watch and then at the door in anticipation of the big moment, but nothing happens... He takes a couple more sips of the Manischewitz Concord Grape wine he is drinking, compliments his cousin Theo on graduating from high school in June, and engages in more pleasant and polite small talk.

At 7:45 p.m, the doorknob finally begins to turn, and Michael immediately signals to everyone that this is the big moment. The music is quickly turned off. Michael had worked out with his mom that the front door would be locked so that the turning of the doorknob would be the indicator to everyone inside the studio to go and hide. All the guests scamper about, quickly trying to identify a space within the cramped room to try to hide. Someone turns out the lights, and silence falls across the darkened room.

The doorknob turns frantically, with a key inserted, releasing the lock. The door slowly opens, and all the guests, on cue, jump out and yell, "Surprise!" However, it is not John, the guest of honor, standing in the doorway; instead, it is only Ruth. She does not attempt to enter but stands there as the door slowly swings open. The illumination from the external house lights bathe her in an eerie silhouette of light and shadows. She is alone, and something does not seem right, as she appears distraught and trembling. "Mom?" Michael asks, "Is everything okay?" He rushes to her side, and once there, he can clearly see that something is very wrong as tears rapidly stream down his mother's face. "Mom, what is it? Are you okay, what's wrong? Where's Dad?" demands Michael, trying to remain calm. All the guests have now moved in and surrounded the mother and son, all with deep concern etched on their faces.

Ruth takes both hands and clasps Michael's face in her palms. He can feel her hands trembling against his cheeks.

"Michael, your father… your father is gone…" Ruth utters in a raspy, barely audible whisper. "Gone? What do you mean he's gone?" Michael replies. Ruth looks into Michael's eyes and says, "Your father and I were upstairs in our bedroom getting ready to come down for the party…all of a sudden, he…he…clutched his chest and fell over… I called for you. Didn't you hear me? I called for you!" she repeats. "No, I didn't hear Mom… I mean, the music down here was so loud… so I… Mom, where's Dad?" Michael asks again, as he suddenly becomes aware of the flashing emergency lights of the ambulance outside. "I told you…he's gone… He had a heart attack… I called 911… but he was already gone…" she says, holding back tears of anguish. Finally, the dam of sorrow breaks, and Ruth screams in heart-wrenching agony, "Oh God! He's gone, what I am going to do… he's gone!" She falls forward and collapses into Michael's arms. The crowd gasps and instinctively and collectively rushes to comfort Ruth and Michael.

Just then, Michael watches in shock and horror as the paramedics slowly carry John's body down the stairs from the main house on the stretcher and pause momentarily as they pass the entrance to the front door of the basement apartment, where Michael and Ruth are still in the doorway. It feels like time has stopped, and everything feels utterly surreal to Michael. Images and memories of his father flash in front of his eyes. Michael feels completely devastated, as he and his dad were so close. He stands frozen, not knowing what to say or do, as he had just talked to Dad less than two hours ago.

John's body is lying lifeless on the stretcher, with a white sheet covering his body and face. Suddenly, an unexpected gust of wind blows up the far corner of the sheet, revealing John's face and the tubes and wires still connected to him that the EMS crew used to try their best to revive him.

Michael feels overwhelmed by the sea of emotions he is drowning in. His mind is racing, and he feels helpless, lost, dazed, and confused. He stands in the doorway holding his distraught mother as the steady raindrops pelt his father's face. The droplets rolling down John's face give the appearance of tears of sorrow streaming down the cheeks of the deceased.

The skies seem more ominous now, and the dark clouds looming overhead appear even more prominent and angrier. The moon peeks out and shines its light, illuminating the dark and empty street.

Meanwhile, as all the guests are intensely focused on Michael and Ruth, no one sees the movement happening in the far corner of the apartment. A menacing-looking, black wisp of ectoplasm levitates from beneath the floor and rises ever so slowly to the top ceiling of the apartment. It pauses briefly, seemingly observing everything happening, and then silently penetrates the ceiling and vanishes. Just before it disappears, Michael, out of the corner of his eye, briefly catches sight of the flash of a shadow and movement in the corner, but when his vision adjusts and he looks closely, he sees nothing, and dismisses it, returning to consoling his grieving mom.

Chapter 1 THE AWAKENING

Michael has moved out of his family's house and now lives in his own small, cramped studio apartment. It has been three months since he made the decision to leave. Although he still lives in Brooklyn, he felt that he needed a change from the painful and bittersweet memories that remaining at the house would continue to bring, and he also felt the need to show some independence and go out on his own. His new neighborhood isn't the best, but the rent is affordable. He has been conservatively living off of his share of a small sum of money that his father left for him and his mother, saved up from his years working in construction.

Of course, he recognized that his departure would mean leaving his mother alone, and although he is concerned for her, in his eyes, it is her house; it was the house that she shared with her husband and raised her family in. So, for all those reasons, he thought it was time to move out and begin his life as an adult.

In his apartment, there is a faded and worn bookcase in the corner, and on its top shelf contains a small USVI flag and a dusty funeral booklet that reads "John Hill, Beloved Husband, and Father." There are unopened past-due bills strewn across the floor. Michael is in a deep sleep in his bed, under the covers, but is tossing and turning, experiencing a terrible nightmare, his eyelids fluttering rapidly, indicating REM sleep.

In his dream, Michael is walking down a deserted street. It is raining heavily with thunder and forked lightning flashing overhead. He moves cautiously through the pitch-black darkness and dampness of the night. He has an unmistakable feeling of being watched, but from where or whom eludes him. The air feels thick with a weighted heaviness that something terrible is about to happen, making him anxious and afraid. He cannot see anything beyond a few feet in front of him due to the pouring sheets of rain.

Suddenly, a man in a black hooded cloak steps out of an alley, a few yards away but directly in front of Michael's path. The man is at the end of the block and stands there, not moving and looking directly at Michael. Michael strains to see the figure amidst the driving torrents of rain. Just then, a flash of lightning illuminates the sky, and Michael briefly sees the man's face, which looks strangely like his father… Michael is frozen in shock and confusion, witnessing the presence of someone resembling his deceased father. The man then turns around and quickly darts back into the alley, with Michael chasing after him. "Wait…Dad? Is that you? But… how are you here…We…We buried you…?" Michael asks and yells simultaneously as he pursues the hooded figure. His anguish and fear slowly give way to the faint possibility of hope that somehow his father has returned. "Is it really you… Dad?" Michael asks. The hooded man does not answer but keeps running, his dark cloak billowing behind him like a cape in the chilly night air.

Michael continues pursuing him, running deeper into the alley, which contains an abandoned warehouse at the far end with an open door. He sees the dark figure go inside the door. Michael is not far behind, and quickly enters the building, and sees the dark figure still rapidly moving ahead of him. Michael continues, breathing heavily from running so fast and wholly soaked from sweat and the rain.

"Dad! Stop! It's me, Michael…Wait…," Michael asserts, but the figure does not stop. "Stop!" Michael shouts again, his voice cracking with emotion. "Please, Wait!" But the man does not slow down. The warehouse is old and rundown, and as he is chasing the hooded figure, Michael notices that rain is streaming into the abandoned building from large gaping holes in the roof, accelerating the internal decay of various wooden boxes and crates rotting within the warehouse. As he runs through deep puddles of water, it starts to occur to him, "What if this isn't my father? What then?" he thought to himself, but then also, "What if it actually is my dead father… What do I do then?" He dismisses the thoughts as he sees the figure dash into a dark room ahead, and Michael quickly follows. Michael enters the room, which he sees is completely enclosed, with no other way out, yet the hooded figure is nowhere to be seen. Michael strains to see and look around in the darkness when suddenly, the hooded figure appears directly next to him, and he is now completely faceless, devoid of eyes, nose, or mouth. The figure's face then begins to shift and contort and now changes to a dark-skinned Black man with a deep scratch or scar on the right side of his face. He extends his left hand, palm up, offering Michael what appears to be a handful of gold coins, and non-verbally beckons him to take them. Michael looks at the man, trying to process the situation and not entirely understanding what is happening. Michael shakes his head, indicating no, declining the offered gold but keeping his eyes squarely fixed on the hooded figure.

The gold coins abruptly morph into a writhing pile of worms and maggots in the man's hand. Michael recoils in disgust at the sight of the vermin and steps back away from the man. The man, whose face is still partially shadowed due to his hood, also remains staring directly at Michael but otherwise remains entirely still and unmoving.

However, this does not last for long, as the hooded figure unexpectedly dashes into a far corner of the room with his back to Michael and faces a wall. Even with the hood on his head, Michael can see the figure breathing extremely heavily and staring at the wall before him. The hooded figure raises both arms above his head and, with his right-hand gestures, circular clockwise. A circular section of the wall illuminates, and the silhouette of dark demonic figures surrounded by fire can now be seen within the illuminated area of the wall. The image looks like a bizarre movie screen, with the characters within the movie all looking directly at him.

There is a sudden sound of rapid, repetitive, and incomprehensible loud whispering all around Michael, saying – "All That Glitters Is Not Gold!" The whispering gets deafeningly louder. Michael covers his ears with his hands. He can't understand what is being said, and the repetition and volume make him feel like he is losing his mind. "What are you saying? I don't understand!" Michael screams.

Desperate for relief, Michael grabs the figure by the shoulder. The figure violently turns around, but now it unexpectedly has Michael's face, which appears distorted, evil, and demonic with sharp, jagged teeth and slanted red, piercing eyes. The figure speaks with a thick, distorted Caribbean accent. "Sometimes de' demon marks you, even before you get the mark for real…Sometimes de' demon marks you in your dreams…"

The figure then raises its now mutated right hand.

Michael instinctively raises his arm, palm up, to block the anticipated blow, and the hooded figure slashes wildly and cuts him deep within the center of his palm, which gushes an extremely exaggerated amount of blood. Michael screams and staggers backward in agony while clutching his injured hand as the room suddenly goes black.

Michael jumps awake from the nightmare, drenched in sweat. Simultaneously, an ominous wisp of black ectoplasm floats in the air and retreats from Michael's bed. The ectoplasm contains the image of a demonic face embedded within embers of fire. It is quickly moving towards the front door, unseen by Michael. The ectoplasm penetrates the door, and when this occurs, Michael suddenly hears a loud knocking and savage scratching and wild snarling from the top of the door, working its way down to the bottom. This startles Michael, but before he can respond, it abruptly ends when the alarm clock and his cell phone begin ringing simultaneously. Michael is disoriented and believes he may have been still dreaming. He immediately looks down at his palm - but he sees no mark. The alarm clock reads 7:30 a.m. Michael stops the alarm, lets the cell phone ring several times, and then answers. "Hello," Michael utters in a confused, raspy, and sleepy voice.

The automated voice on the other end says, "This is an urgent call for Michael Hill, this is South Coast bank, with an important financial matter." Michael angrily hangs up, but the phone rings again. However, this time, it is not an automated recording but a live person on the other end. "Good morning may I speak to Michael please?" says the pleasant business-sounding voice. "Dis' Michael... Who dis?" Michael replies. "Is this Michael Hill?" the voice demands. Michael pauses, then says, "Umm... Yes, who is this?" The pleasant-sounding business voice continues, "Mr. Hill, my name is Amy Collins from the Collections Department of South Coast Bank. Mr. Hill, this is an attempt to collect a debt. The mortgage for your house is currently 15 months delinquent, and I am calling to make arrangements with you to get your account caught up." Michael angrily interrupts, "Yo' this is harassment with these back-to-back calls! I already told y'all," Michael asserts. "The house was left to me by my dead father. It's our family home, I am trying to figure out how I can pay the past due amount, and get caught up, but right now, I don't have the money!"

"Mr. Hill, I understand your situation, and we are here to help. We have several options that can help you avoid foreclosure such as a quick sale...," the bill collector states. "I said No!" Michael angrily interrupts. "Mr. Hill, I really need you to be open to exploring the various options available to you, as I stated, your account is several months past due, is in collections, and may fall into foreclosure unless the past due amount is addressed to bring the account current...," the bill collector asserts. Michael angrily responds, "What part of I don't have the money, don't you understand?" Michael angrily throws the phone across the room, smashing it against the wall. Breathing heavily in frustration, he clenches his fists and glares at the broken phone pieces on the floor. He then leaves and heads to the shower to prepare for work. As he showers, he thinks, "Some mornings, whether you stay in or get out of bed, it just seems that no matter what, if things are destined to go downhill…then no matter what - they definitely will."

Chapter 2 BROTHERS

Michael walks down his Brooklyn neighborhood street. He reaches into his pocket and checks the time on his backup cellphone. He passes the bodegas and stores he grew up with since moving to New York from the Caribbean. Even early in the morning, men stand outside the bodegas on the corner, drinking and talking loudly. As the look and feel of certain parts of Brooklyn continue to evolve and change due to gentrification and other factors in other areas of the borough, some less affluent parts still retain a grittier, unmistakable, more urban feel. This particular neighborhood is one of those, reflecting a close-knit, working-class, primarily Caribbean demographic. As he walks, he looks up at a giant Nagasaki Tires billboard on the side of one of the apartment buildings, which he glances at every day on his way to work.

He walks into the neighborhood's Jamaican/Caribbean Bakery & Restaurant, where he and his friend Buns go regularly to get breakfast. Brooklyn is the Mecca for Caribbean immigrants living in New York and the mainland U.S. You can find a Caribbean national in Brooklyn from literally every island nation. So, it makes sense that immigrants residing within Brooklyn will also naturally gravitate to familiar things that remind them of home, and there is nothing that reminds someone of home more than food. So, within the packed Caribbean bakery are familiar smells of delicious Caribbean baked goods and foods and familiar accents reminiscent of numerous Caribbean islands. Here at the bakery, those from the so-called "big islands" like Jamaica and Trinidad interact freely with those from the offensively dubbed "small islands" like St. Thomas or Antigua – the environment could be viewed as a modern-day biblical Tower of Babel. However, communication is not an issue for the patrons of this establishment, as they clearly understand and communicate with each other utilizing their individual accents. The bakery owner, Roger, even set up a table in the back where the men could play dominoes, slamming the table aggressively but in good fun, with each domino placement, and drinking ice-cold beer whenever they wanted. America is a great melting pot; it can sometimes feel like everyone is an immigrant from somewhere else. Yet, the promise and potential of that rich multicultural mix has always interested and fascinated Michael about living in America. At the same time, immigrants from the Caribbean have historically found strength and protection in clustering together in places like Brooklyn. Businesses like this bakery are an oasis for Caribbean people to come together and get recharged in their culture. To the untrained ear, an outsider may not be able to determine where each person is from, but to the trained ear, you can hear and discern differences in the pronunciations, varying accents, and even the slang or sayings that may be used, and determine each island nation represented.

As Michael is settling in and enjoying the accustomed ambiance of the bakery, a few minutes later, Buns arrives. Buns is also 18 and a second-generation Caribbean-American immigrant, with multiple tattoos covering his entire right arm, and he has an occasional stutter. Buns has ear pods in his ears and is listening to classic reggae. He has a gold tooth on his upper front right tooth. Buns is very intelligent but tends to mask it with his streetwise bravado and a bit of a know-it-all attitude.

"Yo' yo, let me get a beef patty with coco bread and a large coffee," says Michael, addressing the server behind the counter, as Buns walks up to him, and they hug. "My Man! What's poppin' Bro?" says Buns. "Yo,' everything is everything… You want somethin' to eat?" says Michael.

"Yeah, le…le…let me get a coco bread with cheese and a juice!" Buns replies. Once again, addressing the restaurant employee behind the counter, "Yo' hook my man up!" Michael pays for the food, and they begin talking in front of the counter while waiting for the food to be prepared. "Yo' man, on the real, thanks for looking out for me with this job. Matter of fact, today marks my six-month anniversary. I owe you man," said Michael.

Buns looks down as he responds, "Just keepin' it 100 bruh! You don't owe me nothin' playa. We brothers right?" Michael smiles and utters, "Yo' Always!" which is Michael's customary response. The two have been friends since grade school and first developed and utilized the call-and-response greeting they continue to always use when meeting. Buns, being more of the alpha of the two, would usually always lead with "We Brothers, right?" and Michael would make the response - "Yo' Always!" Michael's family is originally from St. Thomas, U.S.V.I. Buns' family hails from Haiti but moved to St. Thomas when Buns was just a baby. The two families eventually became friends due to the close friendship of the children, and finally, both families moved to Brooklyn when the boys were still young, remaining in close contact, attending school in Brooklyn together, and further cementing the close ties that began in the islands.

"For real though, good lookin' out with the job," Michael says. You know things have been tight with money lately, especially with my Pops passing away… The main thing is that I'm trying to help my mom keep the house, which my dad fell behind in paying after his first heart attack. So, by the time he had the second one, they 'bout ready to foreclose on us now… On top of that, I'm lucky to still have my apartment, as I'm also behind on my own rent. So, I got all these damn bill collectors hounding me for money." says Michael. "Sounds like you need to s…s… start playing Lotto bruh – haven't you heard, all you need is a d…d..dollar and a dream." says Buns. Michael scoffs, "I don't believe in all that shit, that's just a scam to take your money."

Buns snap back, "You say that, but imagine if you did win a big jackpot and had all that money. Imagine if y…You could have all your wishes and dreams come true. What would you do?" He pauses and thinks about it for a minute, "I guess, I'd finally start living…" says Michael. Buns presses him for clarification, "Oh, so y…y…you ain't living right now?"

Michael doesn't respond immediately and looks away. "Before my pops died, he was always talking 'bout money…mostly 'bout the money he never had…when he died all he left was debt… It's strange though because since he passed, I keep having the same dream about him over and over again. It's actually more like a nightmare than a dream, and it had me shook dawg!" Michael explains. "Yo' don't trip on that shit man and forget what I said about the L..l.. lotto. Money ain't everything," says Buns. "You think all dem rich people are happy? They ain't happy. They may be comfortable, but there's a difference…" Buns references. "As far as your d…d… dreams - we don't always understand what our dreams or nightmares mean, and as for your Pops, and his passing, if you think about it, death is just a transition to another life - the afterlife…Just dropping some Caribbean wisdom on you son.", Buns pontificates. Michael smiles, "So, what you know 'bout Caribbean wisdom?" They then effortlessly code-switch from their standard African-American speech pattern and slip into their Caribbean-accented dialogue.

"Well, you know what they say about we Caribbean people - all we do is eat curry, we can work some serious voodoo on your ass, and we work eight jobs at once until we eventually drop dead." Michael responds, using his accent, "Well, as a true West-Indian - I have to say that the love of curry is real - believe that! But mi' no vibe wid' no voodoo wickedness, and I definitely don't want to end up working eight

jobs only to drop dead and be forgotten about… I want to make good money right now, working at one good job I like. Real talk!." Buns laughs before responding, *"Brethren, a wha' you talk 'bout? A job you actually like? What the hell is that? Buns asks. "How many p…p… people you know work at jobs they like? It's just a job, brethren. We are all just working for the money - that's it,"* Buns mentions. They now effortlessly slip back into their standard African-American speech patterns.

"Besides, you ain't even no real West Indian anyway, your people from the U.S.V.I. - y'all ain't no real West Indians! I only grew up in the V.I, but I was born in the true Caribbean land! He proudly proclaims. You need to recognize a real island man in de house - "Sac-Passe! Holla!" Buns proclaims. Michael shakes his head, "Yeah, whatever, forget you *Mamzelle!"* (French for lady) He says sarcastically. They both laugh, marveling at and celebrating their second-generation Caribbean pride, heritage, and ability to code-switch and continue their conversation.

"No, but seriously, all I'm saying is that some people think money is the root of all evil, but I think it's actually the opposite. Money on its own isn't evil; I believe it is a lack of and the desire for money that is the true root of all evil," Michael adds. "Some people will even tell you that money can't buy you happiness, but that's what they tell suckers to demotivate them from actually trying to make money.

Let me experience having the money first, and then I'll report back on whether I'm happy or not," Michael states. "True dat!" Buns confers confidently. Michael says, "We are second-generation West Indians living here in America. Don't we deserve our piece of the American Dream too?" Buns responds, "I feel you dawg! That's why until my ship comes in, and until I get my money right, I smoke my weed tha…tha… that makes everything alright…" Michael shakes his head, "You a fool... Here's our food. Let's bounce." They take the food to go and continue talking as they walk out and head to the I.R.T. #2 subway station to catch the train to get to work in Manhattan.

Chapter 3 BOLD ADVERTISING

Michael and Buns exit the subway and walk up the street to the main lobby door of their office building, laughing and joking. As they get closer to the door, they observe Dirk Betancourt, a 30+ tall, blonde, white man with chiseled model features who is always impeccably dressed. Betancourt is Bold Advertising's Senior VP of Account Management, and he is with Tiffany Freeman, an 18-year-old, petite blonde who wears bright red lipstick and dresses overly provocatively for the workplace, with a Marilyn Monroe vibe. Tiffany is the daughter of the company owner, Roger Freeman. Dirk and Tiffany are down the main lobby entrance to the building, in an alcove, whispering and looking deeply into each other's eyes.

"Yo,' hold up. Look over there. Ain't that the VP from the 31st floor, pushing up on Mr. Freeman's daughter?" says Michael. "Yo' you capping," says Buns. "Yo' he trying to hit everything in this damn company with a skirt on," Buns adds. Michael is solemn-faced as he looks at them, "Yeah, but you know her father doesn't go for that. From what I've heard, he's very possessive when it comes to his daughter," says Michael.

"That's why from the look of it, they definitely trying to keep it on the low. What he doesn't know won't hurt him…," says Buns sheepishly. Michael responds, "It's his company…his rules…," says Michael.

Michael and Buns then open the main office building door and walk towards the central elevator bank behind the front security desk. The security guard, Mr. Charleswell, is a 60-year-old African-American male who stops them at the desk as they attempt to jump over the security turnstiles since they don't have their badges to correctly buzz them in.

"Hey! Where are your security badges?" says Charleswell. "I've told you two a thousand times that your security badge is always supposed to be…"

"Yo' come on Charleswell we just forgot our badges at our desks l…l… last night. But you…you… know we work here. So, just buzz us through," Buns demands.

Mr. Charleswell looks at him disdainfully and states, "I will not buzz you through! You know the rules! Company security badges are to be worn at all times on company grounds—you know that! You two are a waste of nine months and can't follow simple rules! I don't know why Mr. Blake allowed you two degenerates to be hired, even in the mail room," Charleswell says.

Looking and referring directly to Buns, Mr. Charleswell continues saying, "And you, stuttering bastard – you completely bring the quality of this company down by the unprofessional way you look, your sagging pants, and that damn glaring gold tooth in the front of your mouth." Buns looks at him with absolute hate and malice but takes a few moments to let what he heard sink in and then unloads loudly, "No, you bring down the quality of the company, old man! You n… n. need to get that stick out yo' ass, and let us go do our jobs, "Mr. ass-fister sir…"

Both boys begin laughing at the inappropriate name Buns calls Charleswell. At this point, a crowd of other employees is building up at the front desk as Michael and Buns are holding up the line, and the other employees need to move past them to swipe their security badges so that they can get into the main section of the lobby where the elevator banks are. Seeing the crowd building up, Charleswell decides to end the argument – at least for now…

"Man, take these damn temp badges, and get the hell out of my sight!" Charleswell yells.

He throws the badges on the counter, and Buns and Michael hurriedly grab the temp badges, swipe them at the turnstile, and walk toward the elevator banks.

Dirk Betancourt and Tiffany Freeman have just entered the building lobby separately, swiped their badges, and joined the crowd of well-dressed employees, all in business suits and related professional attire, standing before the elevator banks to catch the next elevator. Within the group, they strategically stand beside each other but don't look at each other.

Tiffany slowly extends her left hand over and softly strokes Dirk's right hand, flirtatiously tickling his palm, while both continue looking straight forward.

At the same time, Buns and Michael see what is happening, look at each other, and nod knowingly.

Tiffany and Dirk quickly detach their hands as an elevator going up arrives. They step into the elevator along with several other people.

Buns and Michael catch a just-arriving elevator going down to the mailroom, which is located in the basement.

Buns and Michael emerge from the elevator and walk into the mailroom, laughing and talking again. The mailroom is bustling with employees and other regular activities, as mail is being received, sorted, and placed in employee carts to be sent out to the various floors. Buns and Michael walk up to their desks in the center of the room. Their supervisor steps out of his office just as they approach their desks. Mr. Blake is a 60-year-old, physically fit, bald Jamaican man.

"Mr. Hill and Mr. Thomas, can I see you in my office, please?" Blake utters.

Michael and Buns roll their eyes, get up from their desks, proceed to Blake's office, and walk in. Blake closes the door behind them.

"Gentlemen, do you realize what time it is?" Blake asks. "It's 9:00 a.m," Michael responds. "Wrong, it's 9:05 a.m, which means that you two clowns are late again," Blake fires back. "I have told you that I will not tolerate tardiness, so expect to have your pay docked!" he states. "When are you two going to grow up? I gave you both a shot to work here after no one else would hire you because of your past criminal records, which I, of all people, can identify with. I made a conscious decision to help you. However, I gave specific instructions on what I would demand in return!" Blake demands, with spit accidentally flying out of his mouth. "You are representatives of this department! Therefore, your punctuality, conduct, how you look, how you talk, literally everything about you is a reflection on this department, and on me, as the leader of this team, and I will not have my department demeaned in any way, by either of you! Is that clear? I said, Is that clear?" Blake demands.

Both boys mumble under their breath, but when they see him looking at them, they respond loudly, "Yes!"

"Mr. Thomas, you are to pull up your pants, and look professional, not like a damn convict…and I don't want to hear Mr. Thomas being called "Buns" around here anymore. He is to be referred to by his legal name Egbert…Egbert Thomas!"

Michael starts laughing hysterically at hearing Buns' real name. Although he knows his name, it's still weird to actually hear it, as Buns is completely against the use of his name.

"Yo' I told you don't call me that! That's my government name, which I don't respond to. My name is Buns!" He demands.

"Your name is Egbert Thomas! That is how you will be addressed within this building – is that clear?" Blake continues with fiery resolve, not waiting for a response, "When are you both going to start taking life seriously? Not everything in life is a damn joke. You need to start thinking about your career and your life and have a plan regarding your professional growth, either here at Bold or somewhere else. If not, life will just continue to pass you by. Now, leave my damn office, and start your shift!" Blake yells.

Buns and Michael quickly leave the office and go back to their desks, sit down, and begin sorting mail coming in and placing mail to go out in the various floor delivery carts.

After a few minutes of work, Buns mumbles, "Yo' dat dude is sus, and an effing clown if you ask me!"

"But he got a point tho.' Eventually, we do have to get serious – real talk! I mean, I appreciate you hooking me up with this job and all, but I don't see myself working in the mail room for the rest of my life. I want to go to college, and get an education, but while I'm here I want to maximize my opportunities here. I need to make some real paper – know what I'm saying? We need to be on a positive financial trajectory upwards," Michael says.

"A positive what to the what? Look man, all I'm t…t… trying to do is work just enough to get me a fly-ass ride with them drippy Nagasaki Tires and rims playa! That's w…w… why I got this! Ain't it straight fire?"

Buns pulls a platinum and bejeweled fanged mouthpiece out of his pocket, a canine top and bottom dental retainer with exaggerated, sharp fangs encrusted with additional jewels, which he inserts into his mouth and smiles.

"The hell is that?" Michael asks.

"This is my "drip" secret weapon…Dis is my grillz playa! Yo' these joints is fire! I just got them. Had em' custom-made, dawg! I'm still breaking them in, so I keep them in as often as possible. Yes sir, this mouthpiece is my ti…ti…ticket to all the honies - playa! Once I have my grillz in, with my ink on my arm, along with my weed – man I'm set! All I need now is the whip!" Buns explains. "See, it's a formula. Once you get the whip with the drip Nagasaki rims, the grillz, the ink, the weed, and your money is right – then all the honies will come calling! Then I can hook up with that new s…s… sexy-ass Spanish joint they got at the receptionist desk up on the 31st floor! Oh, man. What's her name again?"

"Maria," Michael offers.

"Oh Maria… Maria…," Buns yells out playfully.

Both boys laugh heartily.

"Yeah, I know you sweet on dat Susan chick up on the 31st floor, and she alright and everything, although she acts like her shit don't stink…, but my girl Maria is the joint!" Buns exclaims.

"Yo, keep Susan's name out of your mouth, playa!" "But seriously though, we do need to start thinking about exactly how, we are going to get the fly-ass ride, with the drip-ass Nagasaki Tires. It takes money to do that. So, we need to start making power moves now!"

Buns scoffs, "Okay, Mr. CNBC. I see we're back on that conversation again. Y…y… you know damn well, they ain't trying to hook no brothers up in here…," Buns states emphatically. He adds, "In case you ain't notice, the majority of the Black employees this company has, either work here in the mailroom or in security."

"Yeah, I see that, but we can't let that stop us from wanting more for ourselves," Michael clarifies.

"So, what you gon' do bout it?" Buns asks mockingly.

"Well, I put in an application for the Assistant Apprenticeship Program position that just opened up on the 32nd floor. That's what I'm going to do about it," Michael declares.

"Wha'! Y…y… you ain't tell me nothing bout that!" says Buns.

"Yo' I don't have to tell you everything I'm doing, dawg," Michael clarifies.

"Oh, so it's like that now? So, you think you're better than me or something?"

Michael looks at him with disbelief, "It's not even about that!"

"So, what is it about then? I see how you rollin', you look like you done…s…s..sold out bro…," Buns states.

"Yo' think what you want. But on the real - I'm going for mine. I'm climbing that corporate ladder no matter what…," Michael says.

4 VOODOO MAN

Archie Berry is a 50+ West-Indian man from the Island of St. Barths. He is a Creole Mulatto, with pale white skin and jet-black curly hair. He is the product of an interracial relationship. So, technically, he's really black, but now, living here in America, based on his appearance, he passes for white, with only a few close people knowing the truth. As a young child, he was brought to St. Thomas, where he grew up comfortably among its predominantly Black population, speaking with his V.I. accent and fully embracing Black and Caribbean culture. However, upon relocating to New York, he quickly recognizes imbalances due to race. He sees how institutionalized racism impacts how you are treated and how far you can go – all based on your race, skin color, or zip code. He recognizes the benefits of living as a white man and concocts a scheme and identity to allow him to reap the benefits of being white. As a result, he lives in two worlds. One, where he routinely goes to Westchester

County and frequents a bar called Sage, pretends to be white, and picks up older, lonely, white women who are either widowed or cheating on their husbands. He has sex with them for money, giving them the momentary fake love and attention they are starving for. He has made a pretty good living from his unethical and immoral actions. While at the same time living in Brooklyn, he has also reunited with friends that he knew back in St. Thomas, who have now also moved to New York, which are the recently deceased John Hill, who is Michael's Dad, and Philbert Thomas, who is Buns' uncle. His circle of friends keeps him grounded, and he can be his authentic self and not have to pretend around them. They hang out, drink beer together, and laugh about what Archie is doing, but have always kept his passing for white, and kinky side hustle as a secret. They were the three amigos, three immigrants making their way in the Big Apple. Despite his fair skin, Archie always felt comfortable among his friends and other West Indians. Archie is self-confident and can turn his Caribbean accent on whenever he chooses, so in Brooklyn, those who mistakenly think that he is white and an easy mark, are suddenly shocked and surprised when he opens his mouth. They learn that this is a fellow West-Indian, just a bit melanin- challenged… Archie has been doing well in terms of the money he is making until he, unfortunately, developed a gambling habit and started gambling away more money than he was pulling in, sometimes even resorting to stealing jewelry and cash from the women he sleeps with. Things got really bad, when he racked up a massive amount of debt with the neighborhood bookie, where the word on the street was that the bookie, who is affiliated with known Mafia ties, was looking for him...

So, as a friend, and drawing on his proud Haitian culture, Philbert suggested that Archie go see Scratch, who is the local voodoo man that he has heard good things about, and suggested that the voodoo man would be able to help him get out of debt and get his life on track. So, although Archie is skeptical at first, he visits Scratch, and after about three weeks from his original visit, he has now returned to Scratch's apartment.

The room is primarily dark, musty, and filled with lit black candles of various sizes. A two-bulb light fixture extending from a frayed electrical wire from the ceiling provides additional overhead light and dangles slowly in mid-air. The room is big but cluttered, and the air feels damp and heavy, coupled with various foul and pungent odors, making it difficult to breathe.

Legions of large black flies buzz throughout the apartment, heralding the presence of a demonic infestation. Strange dark markings and symbols adorn the walls, including an inverted crucifix and a five-pointed star. Rounding out the dark contents of the room is a giant black rooster with a bright red comb in a cage in the corner, the skeleton of a ram goat's skull, several human heads on the floor, and a human skull-shaped chalice on a makeshift altar in the center of the room with an urn on it, and a bloody machete stuck into a nearby wall.

On the makeshift altar, there are crafting tools and several handmade wooden boxes, the size of a girl's jewelry box, with various tiny, demonic, and evil-looking faces intricately carved into the top and sides of the wood boxes. The craftsmanship and intricate details on the woodwork on the boxes suggest that the craftsman is well-trained, patient, and disciplined.

Scratch appears out of the darkness of the room, and is dressed in a black hooded cloak. He places on the table an ancient book with a title scrawled in blood and in patois on the cover – "The Book of The Dead." He opens it, his eyes illuminating to a bright white obscuring his pupils, raises his arms with his right-hand gestures, and begins reading a dark incantation from the book. A circular area of a nearby wall begins to illuminate with a faint white glow, revealing a window-like portal to Hell where the silhouette of legions of emaciated and grotesque demonic figures surrounded by fire are seen standing in a long line extending upwards from a burning, desolate, and cavernous pit leading up to the portal.

Within the pit, there is a mixture of naked, emaciated, and deformed humans along with multiple types and species of demons and bizarre mutations and deformed oddities, including winged, gray-skinned, sharp-fanged, succubi, which are flying around in the air, savagely attacking the frail humans. Mutated and carnivorous black crows eye the spectacle from their perch in barren, lifeless trees, looking for any opportunistic morsel that may become available. The demons, humans, and other freakish-looking beings and oddities are in a state of constant disarray and are wailing, screaming, savagely fighting with each other, and also engaging in massive, graphic, inter-species orgies. The screams and cries echo, mixing with the crackling sounds of burning bones and flesh burning in various bonfires. It is a scene of complete chaos and madness – this is Hell… Congo Savanne, a giant, muscular, ram-headed, winged demon, an evil cannibalistic voodoo deity, is much larger than the other demons. He looks on with a sinister and evil grin and points the way to the legions of demons making their way up to the front of the portal. The demon grabs a cow-footed woman who runs past him, snatching her up and savagely biting her head off before completely devouring her body.

On the earth-bound side of the portal, Scratch's eyes are still illuminated by the spell he has cast; he points specifically to each of the individual shadowy demons at the front of the line on the hell side of the portal and invites them to cross over and enter this world.

"Louvri pòt la! (Translation – "Open the Portal!" in Patois) All are welcome… All are welcome… Brothers, I invite you to cross over… cross over… Cross over now into this world, and enter the wish box, a temporary chamber, as you wait to be joined with your human host…," Scratch commands.

The dark demonic shadow that Scratch points to leaps into the air and jumps through the portal. As it enters through the two-way window-like portal, from the metaphysical to the physical realm, it is transformed from a physical demon into an evil spirit, visually represented as a wisp of thick, black ectoplasm with an evil face embedded within flaming embers and flies directly into one of the wooden wish boxes on the table. The eyes of the demonic figures carved into the wooden box illuminate as the box slams shut once the demon is secure inside.

He points at two additional demons and also, welcomes them to cross over into this world, and they enter their individual wish boxes.

He is abruptly interrupted by a frantic knock at the front door. He gestures in a counterclockwise motion using his left hand, thereby closing the portal. His pupils return to their regular brown coloring.

"Fèmen pòt la (Translation – "Close the Door!" – In Patios)" Scratch waits a moment for the portal to fully close and then slowly approaches the front door cautiously.

"Speak!" Scratch demands.

"It's me, Archie," a weak-sounding voice on the other end of the door responds.

Scratch pulls the deadbolt on the lock and opens the door. Archie stands in the doorway; they lock eyes, and both men stare at each other.

Archie continues standing in the doorway, staring at Scratch, then abruptly, without waiting for an invitation to enter, pushes his way into Scratch's apartment. He is carrying one of the wooden wish boxes under his right arm. As he walks into Scratch's apartment, he throws it on the table. His eyes are wide and bulging with fear, with dark circles under them. He looks haggard and tired. His fingernails are bitten down to the quick, and he is trembling. He is wearing a black hoodie and black jeans.

"I can't deal with this anymore. You have to take this shit back… I don't want it…," says Archie, referring to the wish box.

"Did the box give you what you wished for?" asks Scratch.

"Yes but…" Scratch interrupts him.

"Did the box give you everything you wished for!" Forcefully yelling and slamming his hand on a table.

Archie starts mumbling incoherently and begins sobbing.

"Did you put an offering in the box, as you were told to do?" Scratch inquires.

"Well, I…" Scratch cuts him off, "You fucking idiot! I told you that when you sacrifice a person, you must place something that belongs to the person inside the box as an offering, and that you also cannot leave the box empty without a sacrifice for more than twenty-four hours. And you didn't listen, did you? So, without a sacrifice or an offering, the demon is now hungry and angry, and you bring that here…," Scratch yells.

Scratch covers his nose with his hand as he is suddenly overcome by a different foul and rancid odor from the ones already in the apartment, as the overhead light suddenly begins flickering wildly. Archie then drops to his knees and starts to violently spasm and convulse. His neck, arms, and leg bones begin stretching and snapping as he begins to mutate into a demon, with his eyes first turning completely black, and then further turning blood-red as the transformation progresses. Out of his mouth, rows of jaggedly sharp teeth begin to protrude, resembling a ragged-tooth shark, and his fingers becoming elongated and changing to very sharp claws, with an extended sharp index claw, clearly designed for shredding. The lights are blinking wildly now.

He is only partially transformed and still in a quasi-human/demonic state. He rises to his feet. As this is his initial transformation, he is frightened and confused and pulls a Glock-19 out of the side pocket of his hoodie and points it at Scratch. His mouth and jaw stretch freakishly long, and he screams unearthly and starts limping zombie-like towards Scratch.

"Help me, help meeeeeeeeeeeeeeeeeee........."

His voice becomes profoundly distorted and then growling. Archie can't hold the gun straight because his hands are now claws, and his finger is too big to go on the trigger as he transforms. He accidentally drops the gun, which then slides across the floor. He continues to morph, looking increasingly menacing and demonic, and is making aggressive overtures towards Scratch. He angrily overturns the front table and swings at and smashes one of the bulbs suspended from the ceiling light, causing sparks. The single bulb is now swinging back and forth, casting the room into eerie shadows and darkness.

Scratch begins backing up, straining to see into the darkness, trying to see where Archie is. Archie moves stealthily in the background shadows, unseen by Scratch. Archie suddenly attacks Scratch out of the darkness, clawing his chest, drawing blood, and knocking him to the floor. Scratch, bloody and wounded, frantically crawls on the floor, reaches out, and grabs a box of salt that fell from the bottom of the table. He pours a handful of salt into his palm just as Archie grabs him from behind. Scratch turns around, blows the salt directly into Archie's eyes and face, and yells an incantation, which ignites the salt to fire, burning the demon, partially blinding it, and igniting its upper torso in flames. The demon howls in agony and drops to the floor, writhing around to put the fire out, but continues blindly grabbing for Scratch from the floor.

Scratch rolls over and attempts to run, but the demon grabs his leg and bites down his ankle. Scratch yells in agony, grabs a screwdriver from the floor, and plunges it deep into Archie's shoulder. Archie's jaws release the ankle, but he then leaps into the air from a vertical position and lands on top of Scratch, attempting to go for his jugular, but Scratch blocks the bite of the demon's jaws with his arm, screaming in pain as the devil savages his appendage. However, out of the corner of his eye, Scratch sees Archie's gun just to his left, reaches over, yells an incantation to temporarily slow Archie's advances, grabs the gun, and shoots Archie three times between the eyes. Time appears suspended as the bullets illuminated by Scratch's chant are now properly charged to kill a creature from the netherworld like this, whereas regular shots of this caliber would have no effect. Archie falls stiff and flat on top of Scratch, who then pushes the lifeless carcass away.

The demon within Archie exits his mouth as a plume of black ectoplasm with a demonic face embedded within, screaming in palpable rage as it flies into its wish box on the floor. Archie's dead body lies motionless on the floor. The eyes of the hideous faces on the wish box all glow with an eerie light as the demon is sucked inside, disappearing without a trace.

5 MISS ELLA

Michael is on the 31st floor, delivering the last round of mail. It is nighttime, and the floor is dark and mostly empty except for Ms. Ella, a kind elderly African American woman in her late 60s, who is vacuuming outside the corner office, which belongs to Roger Freeman, Founder & CEO of Bold Advertising. Michael walks up to her, but as he does so, he can't help but smile. Ms. Ella was one of the first employees outside of Buns he befriended upon being hired at Bold Advertising. They met when Michael accidentally spilled a can of cola on the carpet in one of the company's executive conference rooms. Michael was petrified at this happening to him, literally on his first day on the job. At the time, he was delivering mail, had headphones in his ears, and casually drank his soda while making his deliveries. He was about to place a package to be delivered to conference room #1 on the 31st floor when he accidentally and clumsily spilled the soda, discoloring the carpet, while attempting to place the package on the conference room table. Miss Ella was cleaning the office next door, so Michael was able to quickly go next door and ask for help. Miss Ella immediately dropped what she was doing, came into the conference room, and scrubbed the stain out, making Michael very happy and essentially making Ella a friend for life.

"Hey, Ms. Ella," Michael says warmly. "Oh, Michael, baby, you startled me. I guess I was so focused on getting this floor cleaned that I didn't hear you walk up. How are you, son?" Ella says as she warmly hugs and greets Michael. "I'm okay. I guess. Just looking at this fancy office you're cleaning. It makes me feel sort of like I am missing something out of life," says Michael. Ella pauses as she studies Michael's face intently, as she can sense that there is something more behind the scenes of Michael's comments. "What do you mean?" Ella asks.

"Well, everything about this office screams money and excess, from the mahogany desk to the gold finishes – everything. Sometimes, I guess I just wish I had it like this. How I grew up, we never had enough…If I had money like this…" Ella interrupts him before he can finish, "Oh, boy, don't you lust after what you see these folks have. You never know what they had to do to get what they have. The Good Book says, Thou shalt not covet thy neighbor's goods – and God knows what he is talking about," Ella states firmly. "Yeah, I hear you,"

Michael weakly offers with an underwhelmed and unconvinced tone.

"Son, these so-called corporate folk, are a special breed. Have you ever seen them coming to work each morning?" says Ella. "On the subway platform in the morning, they are always running, rushing, and pushing, always moving, always in a hurry. Running up the escalators from the train platform, like a herd of goats running uphill, instead of simply waiting to let the escalators bring them to the top… As they come out of the subway, they are now rushing to get their coffee, and then rushing to get into some type of box, either an office, a cubicle, and eventually an early coffin… I often wonder what they are constantly running to or from. It makes no sense to me. I'm an old woman, I may not say a lot, but I see a lot… That's why I'm telling you, don't envy these people," Ella declares.

"I guess that's what people do in corporate America, they rush, dress up in fancy clothes, and act − well corporate… But the benefit to all that,is you get to make a lot of money and live like this…," says Michael, pointing to Mr. Freeman's Office.

"And you think somehow that means something special? Money isn't everything son… Let me show you something. You see this ring here? I've been wanting this ring for years… I put it on layaway a couple months back, and every month I would pay down on it until I was finally able to pay it off," Ella proudly states. "See, I worked towards a goal for something I wanted, and then it paid off. Young folks today don't want to work for nothing, or wait to achieve a goal, all they want is immediate gratification. You have to put the work in to get what you want out of life," Ella clarifies.

"Look, your ring is beautiful, and don't get me wrong, I definitely understand what you're saying. It's just that for once, I wish that I could live the good life that's all," Michael says.

"Like I said, keep working hard, and you will get everything you want. You get out of this life, what you put into it. Another thing, don't ever take shortcuts to achieving your dreams, if you do those things God will bless you with the answers to your dreams," Ella states.

"You really think so, huh?" Michael asks, smiling.

"I really know so! Keep your life right, and God will make a way for you," Ella says.

"Okay, Ms. Ella. From your mouth to God's ears," Michael states, finally giving ground to the wisdom of someone he has come to respect so much. For Michael, Miss Ella is more than just a fellow employee or the cleaning lady. In many ways, the mother-son relationship he has with Ms. Ella is even closer as of late to the one he has with his own mother. From the first day they met, their relationship has taken off to provide Michael with the daily motivation and guidance he needs. If he has a problem, he talks to Miss Ella; if he needs advice, he talks to Miss Ella; if he needs an understanding and sympathetic ear, he talks to Miss Ella. Similarly, Ella, who has no children of her own, has regarded this young man as the son she never had. So, their bond transcends the confines of the typical workplace colleague-to-colleague relationship.

"Always remember that God puts angels in our path to help us on our journey through life," says Ms. Ella. Michael responds, "I know that's right, because you are my angel Ms. Ella…you are my angel…:" They embrace as the warm sentiments and respect they feel for each other are clearly transmitted and received. "Okay, I have to bounce. I mean…umm…leave, to finish the rest of my rounds on the 32nd floor. So, let me go before it gets too late," says Michael.

"Okay, baby. Remember that life is more than just an endless empty pursuit of material things. Always remember that – *all that glitters, is not gold…"* Ella says.

Michael hears her statement but needs help understanding it or responding to it. He has no idea of how profound these words will come to mean for him.

6 WHAT YOU CAN'T UNSEE

After speaking with Ella and completing his mail drop-offs on the 31st floor, Michael now goes to the elevator bank and presses the up button to go to the 32nd floor to complete the last late-night mail run on that floor. The late-night delivery drop-offs ensure that executives and employees have any important deliveries or mail waiting for them when they arrive first thing the following morning. As the door to the elevator closes, he sees his reflection in the polished surface of the inner elevator door.

The door opens, and Michael exits. He has his ear pods in and is lost in classic hip-hop music and his thoughts.

He pushes his mail cart down the various aisles, dropping off primarily in the dark. Each floor has a power-saving feature that turns off the overhead lights if the sensors don't detect movement. So, the floor goes from being entirely dark to patches of light where Michael makes his deliveries. In the maze of cubicles, he carefully maneuvers his cart, delivering packages and letters and nodding to the music. Michael is preoccupied with his current activities and in his own zone.

As he approaches the floor's copy room, even with his ear pods in, he hears strange noises externally… At first, the sounds are muffled and unclear, but as he gets closer, he clearly recognizes exactly what the sounds are…

He pauses for a moment, debating whether or not to investigate. Part of him is tempted to keep walking and ignore the noises, but another part is intrigued to see a little something-something… Michael pauses and leaves his cart, quietly tiptoeing to the copy room.

Michael peeks into the copy room. His eyes widen in astonishment as he sees Dirk Betancourt having graphic sex with Tiffany Freeman. They are both completely naked, and she is sitting and being maneuvered into varying positions on top of the copy machine. They are both high on cocaine being shared and snorted from a saber-tooth-shaped vial suspended from a gold chain around Dirk's neck.

The copy machine is on and set to an automatic print mode, producing color copies of their "activities," faces, and related body parts… Dirk intentionally positions her face, breasts, buttocks, as well as his own private parts on the copy machine glass screen, producing clear images of who is engaging in these acts and precisely what they are doing.

A strobe light effect is produced by the operating light of the copier, partially illuminating the stark darkness of the floor. Copies fly wildly from the machine, going into the air and landing around the small copy room, with some going underneath the copy machine.

Michael's eyes grow wide as he watches intently, but then, as he tries to get closer to obtain a better view, he accidentally trips on an extension cord, pulling down a gold standing lava lamp that is in the corner, which makes a sound as it falls that the V.P. hears. He looks up, and they both lock eyes – but Dirk does not stop his sweaty romp and continues uninterrupted as Tiffany responds in a state of complete euphoria. Michael walks backward and continues to move away, going towards the elevator banks, while Dirk does not break his stare.

Feeling strangely excited and uncomfortable from what he has seen, Michael quickly reaches the elevator bank and frantically presses the elevator down button. He can't shake the image of what he has just witnessed, and his mind is racing as the elevator arrives rapidly due to limited traffic in the building at this time of night. He quickly steps inside, and as the door closes, he sees a reflection of himself inside the elevator doors, except this time, his image seems blurry, which strikes him as odd because this was the same elevator he rode up in, and his reflection was clear then, so why is the reflection in the door blurry now…

Michael frantically presses the ground floor button. As the elevator starts its rapid descent, calling out the floor numbers as it descends, he suddenly realizes that he forgot and left his mail cart in the middle of the floor. He thought, "There is no way that I am going back up there…" The elevator arrives at the ground floor, the doors open, and he steps out, still deep in thought about the mail cart, "should he go back, should he leave it…" Just then, he is startled by a loud voice from the security desk.

"You okay, Hill?" says Security, Charleswell. Charleswell observed Michael looking out of sorts as he exited the elevator. "You look like you've seen a ghost. Are you okay, something I can help you with?" says Charleswell.

"Uh, no… everything is fine…umm…everything is good. Good night, Mr. Charleswell," Michael says. "Good night, Mr. Hill," Charleswell responds. Michael leaves and quickly exits the building.

7 THE PROMOTION

ichael comes in early the following day; he punches in on the bio-metric time clock on the wall, which reads 6:00 a.m, and hurriedly proceeds to his desk to begin work. Before coming in, he went to the Caribbean bakery earlier than usual, too early to meet up with Buns. This happened partly because he had trouble sleeping last night, as he could not stop thinking about what he saw, but more specifically, how Dirk behaved by staring at him like that with that blank, cold, empty look, "who does that?" he thought. "Is this guy some kind of freak or sicko or something? I mean, just enjoy what you're doing, but why would you at the same time be looking at another dude so intently like that," he thought to himself. The bakery isn't even open to the public as yet, but because the owner recognizes Michael as a regular, he lets him in early. As a creature of habit, he orders his usual breakfast: coco bread with a beef patty and cheese, and a bottle of orange juice. He ate breakfast completely alone. After he finishes, he catches the train to go to work.

So, now, as he sits at his desk looking around, he actually can't believe how early it is. He looks at his watch, and it is 6:25 a.m. The mailroom floor is dark for the most part, with no sorting of mail, no gossiping about sports or women, no machines going, no nothing – just quiet darkness.

As he ponders his thoughts, the mailroom manager's office door suddenly opens, and Mr. Blake steps out.

"Michael, good morning, good morning! I thought I heard you come in. Wow, look at the time it isn't even 6:30 as yet, and you are already in the office ready for work. Now, that's impressive!" Mr. Blake blurts out. "Looks like you really took that little conversation we had yesterday to heart, and applied yourself," he says.

Michael stands up from his desk to greet his supervisor. "Umm…yeah…Good morning. I didn't realize anyone else was here… I just figured I'd come in and get an early start on the shift," says Michael as he shakes Mr. Blake's extended hand as he walks over to where Michael is standing. Michael immediately feels a bit weird about shaking Blake's hand, as Blake is a germaphobe and is literally paranoid about shaking hands or touching people in general – and yet today at 6:30 a.m, Blake is now shaking hands and acting like he's ready to kiss babies to get elected to Congress… This is definitely not normal behavior for him.

Blake emphatically states, "Now, that's the initiative I was talking about! I knew you had it in you! That's the initiative of a winner," Blake proclaims with a toothy grin. Michael is perplexed at this point. "Hey, can you please come into my office for a quick second?" Blake asks Michael. "Right now? I was just about to begin sorting the mail," Michael says. "This won't take but a minute," Blake says with a smile.

Michael's paranoia goes into overdrive at this point. "He is definitely not acting like his normal salty personality," Michael thinks. Blake returns to his office door and waits for Michael to come over.

Michael shrugs and then walks over to Mr. Blake's office, but as he walks in, he immediately sees the outline of someone in the shadows of the partially lit office, with his back towards the door. Betancourt turns around, steps out of the darkness, looks at Michael directly in his eyes, and smiles.

Mr. Blake comes in and shuts the door behind him. "Michael, this is Mr. Betancourt, the VP of Account Management on the 32nd Floor.", Blake gushes. "I know who he is…," Michael states dryly. "A pleasure to meet you," Dirk exclaims, extending his right hand to shake hands, and Michael reluctantly complies.

Dirk squeezes Michael's hand very hard, sending a non-verbal signal between the two men that he is an alpha and a strong one at that. However, as he releases from the handshake, Michael notices that Dirk slyly wipes his right hand off on the side of his pants immediately after shaking hands. Michael has the immediate impression based on Dirk's reaction, that it was almost as if shaking hands with a Black man somehow meant that his hand is now dirty, and he had to wipe it.

"I've seen you around, delivering the mail, but I don't believe we've ever formally met. So, I came down here specifically looking for you," Dirk explains. "Is that right?" says Michael dryly, looking at Dirk with apparent distrust in his eyes.

Although clearly identifiable "No Smoking" signs are posted all over the floor and building, Dirk pulls out a cigar from his coat pocket, lights up, takes a deep drag, and purposefully blows the smoke in Michael's face.

"Well yes, I came down to deliver the good news myself!" proclaims Dirk. "The good news is that the board and I have reviewed the application you submitted for the Assistant Apprentice Program, and we… I… have selected you to be the candidate this year to have the opportunity to work in the program," Dirk states.

"Isn't that great news, Michael?" Blake gushes. "And guess what, Mr. Betancourt has already turned in your transfer paperwork to HR. So, everything is already being processed – and you start tomorrow!" Blake yells out.

Michael still looks at Mr. Betancourt straight in the eyes but doesn't say anything…

"So, am I missing something here? I came down here to personally deliver the news of a lifetime, which will be nothing short of

transformational for you, and your response is sort of I don't know —
flat, I don't get it…" Dirk states. "I thought you'd be more overjoyed
by the news. I mean, this opportunity will mean a significant increase
in pay, you'll get to learn everything about Marketing, and of course,
best of all, you'll get to work directly with me! So, what do you say?"
Dirk concludes.

Mr. Blake, reading the room and sensing the apparent friction, quickly
interjects, "Well, of course, he's happy about this opportunity. He's
just a little overwhelmed, that's all," Blake offers.

Michael starts to come back into the moment.

"Yeah. That's right. Just a bit overwhelmed is all…, but this is a great
opportunity," Michael adds.

"Well, of course it is! And that's understandable, that you're a little
shell shock at the moment, might take a couple of minutes for it to
sink in I suppose, but it's a solid offer. So, are you ready to come work
with the big boys?" Dirk adds.

Despite his cautious instincts, Michael realizes that this is the
opportunity of a lifetime; how can he say no to a chance like this? This
is his shot! This is an opportunity that he applied for and got! Michael
hesitates, then finally states, "Yeah, I'm ready to work with the big
boys."

"Brilliant! So, it's all set, then! I'll see you tomorrow at 8:00 a.m. sharp!
Oh, and one last thing, it would be wise to go out and get some new

suits. We dress to impress on the 32nd floor," Dirk says slyly. "Oh, and one last thing, I gotta make sure I say, congratulations again on this promotion. You're the new office unicorn, kid! Let me be the first to say that you're officially beginning your Corporate Climb…," Dirk proclaims, pats Michael on the shoulder, and quickly walks out as Michael is still reacting to his final words. "…Yeah…ummm…Thanks. I guess I'll see you tomorrow…" states Michael, although Betancourt has already left. However, Mr. Blake comes over to Michael and hugs and congratulates his employee, as he is genuinely pleased to see this young man move ahead. Blake gives him the entire day off so that he can go out and buy some new suits and get ready for his big day tomorrow.

8 THINGS GO SOUTH

The following day, Michael walks into the office building lobby at 7:00 a.m. He is wearing a dark navy suit, crisp white shirt, dark blue tie with gold highlights, and impeccably shined black wing-tipped shoes. He is also wearing reading glasses, which are not real but are used as a prop to make himself appear more intellectual. He walks right up to the security desk and presents his security badge.

"Good morning!" Michael says and flashes his security badge.

Charleswell doesn't respond.

"Did you notice that I have my I.D. today? So, you don't have to hassle me about not having it today, because I have it…"

"Yeah, I saw it…," Charleswell says, underwhelmed.

"So, I was selected for the Assistant Apprenticeship Program up on the 32nd Floor..."

"Well, ain't that some shit! Well, good for you. Is that what you looked so frazzled about last night? "Charleswell asks.

"Well, I didn't want to say anything about the position prematurely, you know what I mean?" Michael says.

"Well, congratulations anyway! It's not surprising though, you always had potential; you actually have a brain in your head, unlike that sidekick of yours who is completely from the streets, and has no future," Charleswell states. "You are so different, and smarter than he is. I don't understand why you waste your time hanging around with... Oh wait, here comes the devil now...," says Charleswell as he spots Buns walking through the revolving doors. Buns is shocked, and his mouth drops when he sees Michael dressed in a suit and tie. He walks over to the security desk.

"Yo,' so, what up wid' all dis shit? What's with the monkey suit? You... look like you finally sold out all the way – dawg," says Buns. "And why do you keep hiding s...s... secrets from me? And why didn't you call me back yesterday? I called and texted you several times, dawg! says Buns angrily.

Michael clears his throat and responds, "Blake gave me the day off yesterday and told me to go home and prepare for my new job in the Account Management Division up on 32.

"Yeah, I heard about that via the gossip grapevine… That's why I was calling you, t…t…to congratulate you, but I guess I wasn't important enough for you to answer the phone huh," Buns says forcefully.

"See man, it's not about that. It's just that I had to go shopping to get some new gear for the job, and then my phone died…," Michael begins, but is interrupted by Buns.

"Wait, wait, t…t… time out, time out! Your phone died…and das' the reason you didn't get back to me - Nigga please! See, why you keep disrespecting me all the time?" states Buns angrily.

"Ain't nobody disrespecting you, Buns? So, you mad just 'cause I ain't call you back? You mad over a stupid phone call?"

"No, I'm mad because you acting like you didn't want to tell me at all!" Buns angrily counters.

"Look, I just need to do this on my own, okay?" says Michael.

"Yo,' you s…s… straight up selfish! I got you the job here – me! And y… y… you can't even just tell me what's going on?" says Buns with a scowl.

"I'm not trying to stop you from doing whatever you want! But you need to know that all these motherfuckers up in here are some soulless empty suits! They're straight-up users, yo! So, if that's what you want t…t… to be l…l…like – like them… Then do what you what you gotta do! I was wrong about you; you ain't no brother of mine," he growls. Buns then walks to the elevator bank, aggressively punches the button, and catches an elevator going down to the mailroom.

Feeling dejected on his first day of work, Michael goes towards the elevator banks and pushes the button to go up. The doors open, and Michael presses the button for the 32nd floor. He is alone in the elevator because it is still relatively early. He looks at his reflection in the mirrored surface of the elevator doors, which, for some reason, appears even more distorted than before.

Michael exits the elevator and uses his I.D. card to scan in front of the reader to buzz through the door into the main office area, which is empty. However, he notices that the light in the corner office belonging to Mr. Betancourt is on, and the door is open.

Michael walks to the office.

Mr. Betancourt is sitting in his chair, staring blankly out at the panoramic view of NYC from his executive office, with his back towards the door.

Michael knocks, and Betancourt turns around.

"Michael! Wow, it's 7:00 a.m, great first impression for your first day of work! I like punctuality and initiative! Come in, come in, and close the door. Have a seat, please!" Dirk says in a warm, polite, and welcoming manner.

Michael walks in, closes the door, and sits in the expensive leather chair before Mr. Betancourt's desk. Mr. Betancourt is smiling.

"Michael…Michael…Michael… Well, you're here, so, now, what are we going to do with you?" Betancourt asks. "What do you mean?" Michael asks.

Betancourt's face suddenly turns vicious, and he flips.

"Let's cut the shit, okay! You saw something you weren't supposed to see the other night!" Betancourt says venomously.

"Look man, I didn't see anything, and I don't know anything! I'm only here for the apprenticeship program opportunity, that's it!" Michael quickly states.

"Yeah, you better make sure of that! Or I will get rid of your black ass so fast your head will spin. I swear, if you utter one word about what you saw…," Betancourt threatens.

"Yo,' what is wrong with you? Why'd you give me the job then if it's going to be like that?" Michael asks.

"First off, you people don't deserve shit, least of all opportunities like this!" Betancourt yells.

"*You people…* Who the hell…," Michael begins to challenge Dirk, but Dirk turns up the flames and gets more aggressive.

"Shut up! Shut the fuck up! That thing you saw between Tiffany and I, didn't mean shit to me – it is what it is. She's the owner's daughter, and he is protective of his pure little angel. So, we need to make sure that she remains, at least in his mind, as his pure little angel," Dirk states. "In other words, I'm not going to have you or anyone, ruin my relationship with Roger. So, I better never hear you saying anything about what you saw, or about what I am doing to Mr. Freeman's little angel... So, I'm going to keep you right next to me, so that I can keep an eye on you, and if you say one word – your ass is done! No job, no money, no life, no nothing! You get where I'm coming from?" he says nastily.

Michael looks at him with pure malice in his eyes. "Yeah, I got you…," Michael says reluctantly.

Betancourt smiles, after receiving Michael's confirmation. "Great! So, why don't you make yourself useful, and go get me some fucking coffee!" Betancourt directs. Michael gets up from the chair and immediately walks toward the bathroom.

With Michael now out of the office, Dirk pulls out a comb and mirror from his lower desk drawer, and begins combing and styling his hair, absolutely idolizing himself in an over-the-top display of his vanity and narcissism.

Meanwhile, in the men's restroom, Michael is looking at his mirror reflection and mumbling to himself. "What the fuck have I gotten myself into?" he says aloud.

Michael clasps his hands behind the back of his neck. He is shocked, angry, and confused as he paces back and forth in the men's room.

A voicemail message pops up on his phone. It's from his mother. He presses the voicemail icon on his iPhone and listens to the recording.

"Michael, this is Mom. I just wanted to tell you again how proud I am of you for getting this new job. I want you to work hard and be dedicated. I really appreciate your willingness to help me with the mortgage. The small amount of money your father left behind is barely enough to live on, and nothing compared to the amount of debt he left... I mean, you know, things haven't been that easy financially with him being gone... but I don't want to lose my house..." She begins crying, then composes herself.

"Well, anyway, remember that in life, things that are worth it – are worth fighting for. Make this new promotion work for you, to get you to where you want to go. I'm making your favorite – curry goat with peas and rice, and plantains for you on Sunday. So, please drop by. Thanks for all of your help, son. I'll speak with you later. Love you," the recording ends, and Michael is almost in tears.

Talking out loud to himself and pacing rapidly now.

"Shit! Shit! Want to quit? Can't quit. I can't believe this…," Michael says over and over to himself.

After a while, Michael composes himself and leaves the restroom. It's now 9:00 a.m, and other employees are starting to come on the floor. He makes his way over to his cubicle.

Michael is in his cubicle working on the computer. Susan Jennings, a twenty-something African-American woman, walks up to Michael's desk.

"Hi, excuse me Michael, my name is Susan. Susan Jennings," Susan says, but then she stops talking and looks closely at Michael. "I'm sorry, but you look so familiar, don't I know you from somewhere?" she says.

"Yeah, umm… I used to work in the mailroom. So, I used to deliver mail on this floor…," Michael explains.

"That's right! I knew you looked familiar. That's where I know you from! You're the mail guy!" Susan gushes.

"Yeah, I'm the mail guy, or used to be… I got promoted I guess – So, now I'm the new associate trainee here in the account division…," Michael explains.

"Well, congratulations, and welcome to the team! I work on the creative team, so you'll see me around," says Susan. "But for today, H.R. asked me to check in on you. You'll have a formal meeting with Ms. Hawkins from H.R. later, but they just asked me to help you get oriented. So, it's 8:45 now, and the account team meets every Monday morning with our CEO, Mr. Freeman at 9:00 a.m. to go over what our various account and creative teams are working on. So, we should start making our way over to the conference room now. Mr. Freeman doesn't like anyone to be late," Susan explains.

On the way to the conference room, Susan and Michael pass Dirk Betancourt's office. The door is slightly ajar, and they observe Dirk in the office with Mona, an Asian-American female member of Dirk's account team. It is after an obvious intimate moment as Mona gets up from her knees and wipes her mouth with the back of her hands. Dirk gently places his hand on her bottom as she rises, simultaneously adjusting the zipper on his pants. Michael and Susan see all of this, look at each other, but keep walking. Dirk and Mona, oblivious to having been seen, gather their things and start moving towards the conference room.

In the conference room, at the head of the table, is Roger Freeman, a 60+, well-dressed white man. He is flanked on his right by the leader of the account group, Dirk Betancourt, and his team on the right, and to his left is the head of the Creative Group, Jessica Reyes-Powell, a 30-something talented and outspoken Latina, with her team on the left. Tiffany Freeman is seated on the account team, three seats away from Dirk. Michael is also sitting on the account side at the end of the table. Monitors in the ceiling show staffers teleworking via Microsoft Teams. The meeting room and its occupants are the embodiment of materialism. The Account group, all impeccably dressed in business suits and ties, are on the left side of the table, and the creatives are equally nattily dressed in trendy business casual attire on the right. Their pre-meeting conversations are generally shallow and meaningless, and all meeting participants sport the latest technology, including Apple watches, laptops, and a Starbucks coffee cup in front of each of them. Everything is decadently shallow – and perfectly corporate.

"So, what are we working on today, folks?" asks Roger Freeman. "Roger, we are confirmed to pitch the Nagasaki Tires account on Thursday. They were previously represented by BBDO, but they lost the account. I heard, it wasn't a happy separation," Dirk gushes. "The word on the street was that Nagasaki wants a fresh and new approach as to how their tires are marketed in the U.S. So, they are looking for new representation. I'll just add that this account is one of the biggest accounts being actively pitched by various agencies right now, and we get our opportunity on Thursday. So, we have to be ready," Dirk emphasizes.

"With that said, my team has been working feverishly on generating creativity for our pitch. We have a few concepts to show you today," says Jessica. She presses a button on a remote she has, and the large screen on the other end of the screen comes on, with the 1st creative slides already teed up. "We story-boarded all of our concepts, but also moved forward with generating a simulated commercial, depicting three potential concepts. So, our first concept is more traditional," Jessica says.

The presentation continues for what feels like hours. As she comes to her final presentation, Jessica offers,"…and it features the tires in a standard automotive-style ad, where we see a sexy red sports car outfitted with Nagasaki Tires."

The mock ad runs, but when it is done, the room is quiet, and everyone seems unimpressed.

"So, there we go. Those are our three concepts. So, thoughts, reactions?" Jessica asks.

The room is still basically quiet.

"Don't get me wrong, Jessica, I mean I like the ideas, but it just seems like we've seen all of these concepts before," states Roger.

"Yeah, I completely agree with that. Using flaccid textbook concepts, we'll never land a major account like this; it's simply "*no bueno mujer*…," Dirk sarcastically adds.

Jessica shoots him a wicked look. Roger notices it and quickly interjects.

"Folks, we don't have much time. Today is Tuesday, and team Nagasaki will be here on Thursday for the pitch. So, it looks like we will all be putting in a lot of late all-nighters this week in preparation for the pitch. However, for starters, I'll need to have some new concepts coming from both the account and creative sides on my desk by noon," Roger states.

Everyone gets up from the table and heads back to their desks and offices.

Shortly after, Dirk sticks his head out the door and motions to Michael.

"Hey, get in here!" Dirk barks.

Michael winces when he hears Betancourt's voice. Michael reluctantly gets up, walks to the office, and enters.

"Shut the fucking door behind you and sit down!" Dirk nastily orders.

Michael pauses, takes a deep breath, and then closes the door.

Dirk gets up close in Michael's face and starts screaming at him.

"Look, if you're going to be part of my team, I'm going to need you to start stepping it up in terms of your input and contributions to this team! You saw what happened in there – we need new ideas for this account! So, I need you to go back to your little desk and make a list of several concepts we can pitch on this account! I need to see whether or not you can really cut it as a member of my team or not.

I expect to see something from you by eleven this morning! You got me, now get out!" Dirk yells.

Michael does not say anything, gets up, walks out of the office, and returns to his desk feeling completely confused and dejected.

Employee James "Jimmy" Flannigan is an 18-year-old, blond, Irish-American who sits in a cube across the way from Michael. He overheard Dirk screaming at Michael in the office and is staring at Michael with a smile on his face.

"Dude, he's all over you like a cheap suit laddie…," says Jimmy mockingly in an authentic Irish accent.

"You noticed?" states Michael.

They both look up as they hear Dirk still angrily swearing, talking to himself, and throwing furniture around his office. Michael begins crafting the email of ideas for Dirk, but looks at Jimmy, as he begins typing.

"He always this cheerful?" Michael asks.

"Yeah, and believe it or not this is actually a good day for him. Trust me when I say that it won't get much better than this with him, only worse…" Jimmy responds.

Michael shakes his head in disbelief.

Jimmy, seeing that the wind has been knocked out of Michael's sails, says, "Hey man, you look like you could use a quick pick me up – a little nose candy perhaps? Want a toot?" says Jimmy, holding the saber tooth pendant on the gold chain around his neck.

Jimmy takes a snort of the cocaine and offers some to Michael. Michael instantly remembers that Betancourt had a similar saber tooth-shaped cocaine holder on a gold chain as well.

"So, it's like that up in here? And what's up with the obsession with fangs here? "Do all y'all have them matching saber-tooth shaped coke dispensers around your neck?" asks Michael.

"A couple of us do… It's sort of a club thing…," says Jimmy.

"Some club… Y'all party all times of the day, huh? I mean, it is still morning…," Michael adds cheekily.

"Hey, it's cool man… Look, it's like after the pandemic, when most of the country and corporate offices were all closed, then finally started re-opening, and our company employees began slowly coming back, a few of us who came back, just got together and said that we needed a little something extra… We felt like we needed to do something to keep us going through all the suffering that we went through with covid, and some people are still going through. You see, I look at it like this. The pandemic was like *The Blip*, in the Avengers movie. You know, where Thanos snapped his finger, and a large swath of the human population of the earth simply vanished...

At the end of everything, some of those people came back and some of them didn't'…, but for those that did come back, things were very different… So, for me and others who started coming back into the offices, we found that our work environment had become very different, many offices were still empty, endless meetings in front of countless screens, poor work-life balance, some people quiet-quitting – you get the point. So, things are just different now, in terms of the way we work. So, I guess some of us just found it necessary to develop creative ways to adapt to all the changes, and this is the new normal for the workplace," Jimmy explains.

"Honestly, most of the executives here are doing one type of pharmaceutical or another, including your best friend Mr. Wonderful in there. How else do you think we deal with all the work-related stress? I mean there comes a point where, standing around the water cooler talking about what we did over the weekend, as the highlight of my day just ain't cutting it no more…" says Jimmy.

"Yeah, I guess it just never occurred to me that blow, would become the breakfast of champions…," counters Michael. Jimmy laughs.

"You killing me, man…you killing me, says Jimmy, laughing heartily." Trust me, you're going to need it after dealing with Prince Charming in there," Jimmy says.

"Sounds like you're speaking from direct experience on this," Michael says.

"Let's just say, I've had my share of run-ins with him. Everything from his everyday violent screaming and yelling to his passive-aggressive behavior, where he would suddenly stop talking to me for weeks, for reasons only he knows; to publicly shaming me on group emails, and frequently undermining and nit-picking at my work; I mean, honestly, from day to day you're really never quite sure which Dirk you're actually going to get – But other than that, he's a real peach to work for… Right now, I'm waiting to see if he is going to promote me, as he promised to Director, or if I'm going to be passed over again…," Jimmy volunteers.

"So, what are your chances?" Michael inquires.

"Well, let's see, I'm qualified, experienced, and been here for several years now without a promotion or a raise. But, I'm going up against one of the many women he's sleeping with here in the company…," he clarifies.

"Sounds like your job and your chances are all pretty shitty," Michael says.

"Yeah, welcome to corporate America!" Jimmy counters.

"I don't get it. Why don't you just report him to H.R.? He's an asshole! I know there are a ton of functional psychos masquerading as leaders and employers within corporate America, and that sack of shit in there is clearly one of them, so why tolerate him?

You know, I heard somewhere that people don't actually leave their jobs; they leave the problematic people at their jobs. This whole fucking department is a textbook example of a completely toxic, dysfunctional, and hostile work environment," Michael states.

"Hey, please, don't hold back, tell us how you really feel…but also don't be so damn naive. H.R. won't do anything about him. All they care about is ensuring that the company is profitable and legally protected – that's it. H.R. along with the senior leadership of the company is completely aware of what he's doing. They've received numerous complaints about him, and all they've done is just given him some mild taps on the wrist. Trust me, they're fully aware of everything…," Jimmy states.

"Gimme a fucking break…Michael states. Jimmy shrugs and smiles.

"Hey, a few of us are going out for a couple of beers tonight at that bar on 57th Street called "Shenanigans," you should come with us - for a drink; it'll be a blast! While you're there, maybe you could give me a few pointers on women. I'm trying to score a date with Tiffany," Jimmy says.

"Tiffany? As in Tiffany Freeman? Mr. Freeman's daughter? Michael asks.

"Yeah, you know her, man? Oh my God, I really…really… like that girl. I mean, I worship everything about her, the way she looks, even the way she smells…but the sad thing is she doesn't even know I exist…," says Jimmy introspectively.

Before Michael could respond, Susan walks up to his cubicle. Michael finishes the email for Dirk and hits send. Susan walks up, "Ummm… Excuse me, guys, I hope I'm not interrupting?"

"No, no, not at all," says Michael.

"Ummm… Michael, I just wanted to come by and apologize for the small bit of craziness that you saw in the meeting… Please, don't let any of that discourage you," said Susan.

"Yeah, I was beginning to wonder about that, but there seems to be a lot of *cray cray* up in here…," offers Michael looking at Dirk's door.

"I take it you mean Dirk?" she says.

"No, I mean Dick…Cause he's a dick…," Michael corrects her. They both laugh in unison.

"I mean, that dude has serious mental issues. I never really had to interact with him directly when I was in the mailroom, and he's supposed to be my boss now and all, but I still keep wondering why they don't just fire his ass," Michael states.

"Yeah, I guess he's the goose that laid the golden egg. He's landed several high-profile and lucrative accounts for the firm, which has made Freeman and the company board and shareholders tons of money. In fact, Mr. Freeman thinks of him as, well as sort of a son… So, I think they just sort of look the other way, as long as the money keeps coming in," she confirms.

"That's effed up because he needs to get his attitude adjusted, which ain't going to happen if he's viewed as untouchable. If I were in a position like his, I would never behave like him, or treat people the way he does," Michael asserts.

"You got my vote for President!" she jokingly adds.

Michael asks, "No seriously, how do you deal with him?"

She pauses before responding, and then offers, "I guess I just try to stay as far away from him as possible. I mean, I'm new here, and as you saw, he sort of has a thing… a reputation with female employees, where you basically have to sleep with him to get promoted…," she states.

"Well, I definitely would not want to see you have to do that…," he tells her firmly. Michael hits send on several ideas that he sends to Dirk.

She smiles and flirtatiously places some loose hair strands behind her ear. He notices how gorgeous she is. They are both looking into each other's eyes, and you can tell there is an unmistakable spark, chemistry, and attraction there.

"Well, look at me jabbering away… I should go now… back over to my cube. So, maybe I'll see you later?" she says.

"Yeah, most def. I mean definitely…," Michael adds.

She walks away, and Michael watches her mesmerized as she walks away.

Michael looks at his watch. It's now 10:30 a.m. He stares at his watch and then back at a blank computer screen.

An email from Dirk pops into his inbox

The email is in all caps and placed in bold red font:

"I AM SHOCKED! IS THIS THE BEST THAT YOU CAN DO? WHAT THE FUCK IS THIS? YOU SIMPLE SON OF A BITCH!!! ARE THESE THE BEST IDEAS YOU CAN COME UP WITH, YOU FUCKING MORON?"

Michael opens the email and can't believe his eyes when he reads it. Dirk comes storming out of his office. Michael stands up from his desk as Dirk approaches.

Yo,' who the fuck you think you're talking to… What's wrong with you? I am not going to take this kind of bullshit from you!" Michael asserts.

"You'll take whatever I tell you to take! At least if you want to keep your job… See, I run the show here! You got that? You just showed me that you clearly don't have what it takes to be here on the 32nd floor and be a member of my team! You need to start packing your shit up, and preparing to go back to the mailroom, as you probably won't be around much longer after lunch. Thanks for nothing," Dirk states.

Michael sits down at his desk and buries his head in his hands. He has been fighting off a headache, which has been threatening to take over for quite some time now. By the pounding in his temples and the tenderness of his head, it feels like he has lost that battle.

Michael is feeling angry and confused by Dirk's treatment. A calendar invite pops up in his inbox for a mandatory account management team meeting in the conference room.

Tears angrily well up in his eyes at the thought of dealing with Dirk again.

He picks up his laptop and makes his way to the conference room.

Dirk walks behind Michael, catches up to him, and from behind begins touching Michael's back, seemingly to remove a piece of lint from his suit jacket, but he then actually shoves Michael very forcefully. Michael recovers, does not fall, and spins around with a clenched fist.

"Hey, whoa…easy Trigger… You just had a piece of lint, or something, on your back, and I was just removing it. See…," says Dirk, with an obvious smirk on his face.

Dirk, smiling, holds up a small piece of fluff. Michael looks at the fluff, looks at him angrily, turns around, and walks into the room, followed by Dirk and the other team members. Michael sits in the far corner of the conference room table, as Dirk begins the meeting.

"Okay. So, first I am going to start with a bit of housekeeping and announce that our team member Mona Kim has just been promoted to the position of Director," said Dirk.

Jimmy looks down at the floor, bitterly crushed, humiliated, and disappointed at being passed over yet again for another job opportunity.

Mona Kim is the twenty-something Asian-American female that Michael and Susan saw in Dirk's office after an apparent sexual encounter of some type.

The other employees half-heartedly clap to congratulate Mona, seated at the table.

"So, let's go around the table, and have each team member discuss what projects they are working on?" says Dirk.

They go around the room.

It finally comes around to Michael's turn.

"Me… Well, I um… just started. So, with the exception of brainstorming for the Nagasaki meeting, I haven't really gotten into much else as yet…," offers Michael.

Dirk forcefully slams his fist down on the desk, startling everyone in the room. Buns has just arrived on the floor and is pushing his mail cart as he nears the conference room. He hears the commotion and can sense the tension in the room as he looks through the glass walls. Even from outside, and not hearing exactly what is being said, he can still tell that things are definitely not going well for Michael. He pulls out his cell phone and calls his uncle.

Dirk gets up from his chair and begins pacing around the conference room. "You see folks! This is exactly the type of low productivity I am talking about! I need go-getters on my team, not slouches! What do you mean you're not working on anything, when there is so much to be done!" says Dirk.

Michael is stunned and taken by surprise by this unexpected attack… Buns ends his phone call, moves away from the window, and walks towards Betancourt's office.

"You think I got to where I am by not taking the initiative from day one? The excuses given by this man are absolutely ridiculous, and shows that this low-energy schmuck does not have the muster or drive required to make it in this competitive environment. As a matter of fact, you know what, moving forward, I want everyone in this room to stay completely away from Mr. Hill. So, if you see him coming down the hall you walk the other way, if he is seated at a table, you sit at another table. I don't want him contaminating the productivity of this team. Let it be known that our team will excel, despite Mr. Hill...," Dirk concludes, standing just a few feet away from Michael, who is seething with anger

Employees in the meeting are avoiding direct eye-contact with anyone and becoming noticeably uncomfortable with Dirk's overt, aggressive, and inappropriate attempt to publicly humiliate Michael, and are shifting uncomfortably in their seats – but don't dare say anything...

Michael is fuming in his seat and staring angrily at Dirk. Buns having completed his call, walks up to the conference room door and abruptly enters the conference room, and interrupts Dirk by deliberately stepping in between Michael and Dirk.

"Ummm... Ex... ex... Excuse me...Mr. Betancourt, sorry to interrupt, but H.R. just sent me up here to get Mr. Hill. He is needed at home right away due to a family emergency," Buns says.

Buns immediately places his back to Dirk, blocking his view of Michael, looks Michael directly in his eyes, and silently mouths the words...

"Let's get the fuck out of here now!" says Buns, as Michael reads his lips, and packs up his laptop.

Buns escorts Michael out, pushing him out of the room, but as he passes Dirk, Buns looks directly at him and mumbles…

"Change your lifestyle bruh…"

Betancourt glares at Buns as they quickly exit the conference room and go straight to the elevator bank and into a waiting elevator, Buns leaving his mail cart behind, with Michael's laptop in it. As the elevator arrives on the ground floor, the two erupt from the elevator and quickly go towards a backdoor exit leading to a loading dock at the back of the building.

9 THE PLAN

ichael is still fuming and pacing back and forth, pounding the balled-up fist of his right hand into his left. "I knew that motherfucker was up to something… He purposefully set out to publicly embarrass and humiliate me in that meeting…," he says with tears of anger welling up in his eyes.

"Yo,' so what's really going on, man…? You just s…s… started this job, and you got all this drama happening?" Buns asks.

Buns takes his grillz from his jean pockets and puts the jeweled oral appliance into his mouth. He then pulls out a blunt from the pocket of his mailroom smock, lights up, takes a deep drag, and blows the smoke out through the jeweled fangs of his grillz.

Michael erupts, "Yo' I can't take this shit anymore! This man yells at me for no reason, curses at me, and disrespects me every chance he gets… He even sends me nasty emails in all caps, in red, bold, and with exclamation marks! It's as if he's yelling at me even in a damn email – Who does that? And then earlier, that bastard tied to put his hands on me! He fucking pushed me from behind in the hall. I tell you, I should have nailed his ass right there! Then just now, in the conference room, the way he acted, in front of all those people… This is crazy, I don't deserve to be treated like this! He doesn't know me like that," Michael screams, with large globs of spit flying uncontrollably out of his mouth.

"Yo' calm down, dawg. First of all, people don't need to know you or need to have an excuse or reason to not like you or treat you bad. Not everyone is g…going to like you, that's j…just the way it is. De' old people had a saying, that happens because his demons don't agree with your angels…But, with this guy, I could have told you that it would be like this from day one – this guy is a notorious asshole. Things aint going to get better with him, it will only get worse…He has a h…h…history of mistreating people within the company... This is what I was trying to tell you before in the lobby, when you first told me you got the job. But, for real though, if that's how he's t… treating you, dat's effed up… So, wha' you gon' do - quit?" says Buns.

"No, I can't right now. I have to help my mom out financially, especially with the mortgage. Things are really tight, like I told you. So, right now, I really need the money," Michael says in a lower-toned voice. "Maybe I should go talk to H.R…." Michael adds. "Yo, they ain't gonna do nuthin'! Old man Freeman, H.R already know about him, they've received numerous complaints about that guy, and they don't do shit! So what makes you think they are suddenly going to do something now for you?" Buns asks.

Michael looks away from Buns. Although this would be an appropriate opportunity, Michael does not tell Buns about the indiscretion he observed between Dirk and Tiffany as the potential cause of the mistreatment.

"Look, I get what you're going through, but see, the thing is, just like how you just said that you need the money, and that's why you can't quit. He also knows that you n…n… need the money. So, this is exactly why he feels he can treat you like this: he figures that you need the job too bad to leave. Bro, from everything you've told me, it sounds to me like you're also being bullied…" Buns said thoughtfully.

"Bullied… The fuck you talking about, we ain't on no grade school playground…," says Michael.

"No, I'm serious, workplace bullying is a real thing – and you're being bullied! I saw it on an old episode of Dr. Phil on YouTube the other night. Believe it or not, bullying happens to adults too, especially at work. On the real, that was the other reason I was calling you when I heard you got the job, was to t…t… tell you that Betancourt is an asshole, and working for him is hell," says Buns.

"According to the show, you are dealing with someone whose bullying energy is completely focused on you. They said bullies come in all forms – men and women, and make no mistake, you are the t…t… target. He will embarrass, humiliate, and isolate you, all to break you down. S…s…so, he will come at you aggressively, or even passive-aggressively, and give you the cold shoulder and silent treatment at one time, and then scream his head off at you at another. He is a broken and unhappy person. He is also a narcissist, insecure, lacks empathy, and enjoys abusing people. Something probably happened to him at some point, which turned him like this, where he looks to victimize other people. What do they say, hurt people – hurt people, right?" Buns says.

"People like him survive by burying themselves deep within a company's structure. They are good at what they do and therefore are needed, or they find other w…w… ways to secure their longevity. Corporate bullies target people they identify that they feel they can intimidate or push around. Any of this starting to s…s… sound familiar?" Buns asks.

Michael's face shows what Buns describes, precisely what he has been going through.

"Yo,' I ain't no punk, and I ain't taking his shit no more!" Michael said.

"Ain't got nothin' to do with being a punk. The b…b… bad part about it, is that the micro-aggression and treatment eventually spill over to the employees within the environment who see him disrespecting you, and then they will, for their own survival, either distance themselves from you, or begin disrespecting you themselves… Some of them may even b…begin agreeing with his treatment, take his side, and even try to become friendly with him, like some kind of bugged-out Stockholm Syndrome shit or something. On the video, it said that you have to s…s… stand up to him, but acknowledges that if you do, there will be retaliation. They said if you try all of that, and it still doesn't work, or even gets worse, then your best bet is to quit," Buns says.

Michael quickly responds, "I told you I can't…"

"Okay, I feel you… Well, we could put on hoods and beat him down in the street, but he'll snitch that it was you, and you'll still lose your job anyway, or another idea is – you could get that kid "fixed…," Buns states sheepishly.

"What do you mean, *Fixed*?" says Michael hesitantly.

"Fixed," as in go down to the voodoo man and get his ass "fixed" so that he can't fuck with you no more, but no one can trace it to you…," Buns states.

"Voodoo? You're joking, right? "You actually believe in that shit?" Michael says.

"Yeah, I do, and I'm dead serious. Every race and culture has their own v… v… version and belief in the occult and magic. For us, as Black Caribbean people, voodoo is just one of ours," Buns states.

"How do you know so much about this shit?" Michael asks.

"Well, it's a part of my culture, right – being Haitian, and that's not to say that it's a thing that every Haitian agrees with or even believes in, but I do, and I have personally been studying the occult and voodoo for a while now. I know I never mentioned it to you before, and I don't really talk about it, or practice it, or anything like that, but I r… r.. respect it as a way that Black people for centuries have culturally used magic to make their wishes come true or change their situation. It's like there's good magic and bad magic. I'm into good magic," Buns states as if he were lecturing on the topic, and then continues, "Remember that before slavery, Africans had their own religions, and voodoo is an off-shoot from that" Buns points out.

Voodoo is culturally rooted in worshipping nature and the ancestors. It's about living in peace and doing good. However, voodoo is constantly vilified in America and Western culture and is only shown in movies and TV, as a damaging practice. But the t…t… truth is if you need help with money, want your business to flourish, or even protection from a mean boss…magic could be used for all of that. I'm talking about protection or good magic – not evil magic," he clarifies.

I'm not saying it can't be used to do bad things, but my family is not into that. I got hooked on it from my Uncle Philbert. He had this one guy at his job who kept fucking with him, so he w…w… went to the voodoo man down on Nostrand Ave. and got his ass "fixed!" after that – no more problems. He had another close friend named Archie who was having money problems and went to the Voodoo man, and after that, we haven't seen him since; my uncle says he's living on easy street now…," Buns concludes.

Michael scoffs at Buns' suggestion, "C'mon man that shit ain't real. All that hocus pocus, mumbo jumbo is just the power of suggestion…"

"No, dude, I'm tellin' you it's real. Look, the bottom line is Betancourt ain' gon' stop messin' wid you – unless you stop him first… I'm telling you, the d…d… dude who was messing with my uncle ultimately backed da' fuck off – real talk. I know where he lives – I know where the voodoo man lives… We could go there right now. He charges $500 for the first visit. If you don't have that on you, I can spot you, and you can pay me later. I mean, based on what you going through, it's w…w… worth at least checking out… What do you really have to lose? And I already called the Uber… and our driver Pash, in a black Corolla, will be here in exactly six minutes…So, whatcha' gon' do?" Buns says, smiling.

Buns is persuasive and makes a compelling argument by phrasing it as a "what do you have to lose proposition," which is a bit of a manipulative strategy he has always used on Michael since they were in grade school. He knows that he can get Michael to do the things he wants him to do by literally covering all plausible outs from the argument, making it difficult for Michael, who tends to reason everything out to say no. Michael pauses and thinks about what Buns is suggesting.

"Yo' fuck it then - let's go! At this point, I am open to trying anything, and like you said, I got nothing to lose…but this shit with this guy has to stop one way or another, cause I'm not going to live my life like this."

10 THE WISH BOX

The Uber pulls up, and both young men exit the car. The Uber barely waits for them to close their doors before he takes off due to the driver's concerns for his safety, as the neighborhood is not the best. The buildings in this area scream for revitalization or demolition, whichever can come first. To say that the neighborhood is economically depressed would be a gross understatement.

"You sure this is the right place? This place looks jacked up...," Michael states, looking around.

"Yeah, it's the right place...," Buns says.

Looking at the bombed-out building they are directly in front of.

"So, what apartment is it?" Michael asks, feeling skeptical about why he agreed to do this.

"He lives in the basement," Buns says.

"Okay. So, let's go...," Michael states and starts advancing forward, but notices that Buns isn't moving...

"So, about that... My uncle said I can't go in with you because the voodoo won't work. The v...v... Voodoo man has to work with you in private." Buns explains.

"Yo' I ain't going in there by myself! You brought me down here to this God forsaken place, and now you're trying to back out of it?" Michael responds angrily.

"I'm not b...b... backing out, it's just that in order for this to work, you have to go in and do it on your own, that's all... Look it's going to be alright. My uncle called and set everything up...So, he is expecting you. Here's the money you need." Says Buns pulling out a fat wad of twenties from his pocket, tied together with a dirty rubber band. "You can get that back to me later... Just b...be cool man...relax... and go handle your business... His name is Scratch," Buns says.

"Scratch? What's his real name? I ain't going up in there calling some random dude - Mr. Scratch", Michael offers with a lot of attitude.

"Not Mr. Scratch, jackass..." Just Scratch..." I don't know what his government name is...People say he m..m... moves around a lot, never in the same place for long. They say he was born in the Dominican Republic, but grew up bad, committing horrible crimes at a young age, who was being pursued by the police. So, to escape, he snuck across the border, and grew up in Haiti, where he was trained in voodoo. At some p... point he moved to France, and did hard time in jail before coming to America, living in South Florida first, before coming up North to New York. My uncle says he's the real thing about voodoo." Feeling like he provided all the information he needed, Buns concludes with, "They say he helped a lot of people. Um…one other thing - you gon' need this…"

Buns reaches into his jacket's inner pocket and pulls out Betancourt's comb with strands of Betancourt's blond hair in it.

"The hell is this?" Michael asks.

"When you were in the conference room in that meeting with Betancourt, before I came in, I called my uncle, and he told me what to do…," says Buns, pausing a bit before continuing. "I w…w..w… went into Betancourt's office when no one was looking and took it…," he explains.

"You broke into his office and stole a fucking comb?" Michael asks, not believing what he's hearing.

"Not for the comb – for his hair… Scratch will need the hair from the comb…and by the way, I didn't break in… I j…j… j just obtained entry using alternative methods…," Buns says slyly.

"Get the fuck out of here! Yo' you're nuts…this whole fucking thing is nuts! I'm not going in there. Let's just forget about it - this is ridiculous," Michael insists.

Buns defensively cut him off, "No, w…w… what's ridiculous is that you're being bullied by another man, who won't stop d…d… d… disrespecting, mistreating, and harassing you – and gets off on it… That's what's r…r…r. ridiculous! Do you want to keep living like that? Just even the playing field and teach him a effin' lesson. Get him "fixed" – problem solved!" Buns concludes.

"Fuck!" he yells out. "All right. All right! Give me the damn comb!" Michael grumbles as he snatches the comb from Buns.

"Yo' just wait for me here," Michael hisses.

"No doubt, I'll be right here when you come out. Handle your business! Yo' we Brothers, right?"

Michael waits a moment, then reluctantly responds to the call-and-response phrase the two friends frequently use.

"Always," Michael says.

Michael walks into the building as the exterior door has been left open. The building looks like it should be condemned. The lobby has faulty and exposed wiring, and rats and roaches are actively running about. The stench of stale urine permeates the building, and there is the sound of babies wailing behind one or more of the closed apartment doors. Michael sees the staircase door, opens it, and walks down it. He then proceeds down the long, dark corridor to a door on the left and knocks on the door. A tall, dark-skinned Black man with a scratch or scar on the right side of his face partially opens the door and peaks through the space between the door and the doorframe.

"Speak!" the man utters in a voice full of deep bass.

"Ummm… Looking for Scratch…," Michael responds.

"Who it is?" the man asks, his phrasing giving away his Caribbean roots.

"Buns' friend… I mean Egbert's… friend. His Uncle Philbert told me to come see you… He said they called you?" Michael explains.

Scratch closes the door, removes the security chain, and slowly opens the door.

"Yeah… I've been expecting you… Come in," Scratch states.

As Michael walks in, he looks at Scratch's face. He immediately gets the feeling that he feels like he has seen Scratch before but can't remember from where… The place is dimly lit and is a mess, with furniture knocked over and items all over the floor. He notices a painted image of a red upside-down cross painted on the far corner wall and that there is a table with tools and multiple medium-sized handmade wooden boxes with various tiny, demonic, and evil-looking faces intricately carved into the top and sides of the wood boxes. However, on one of the boxes, the eyes of the minor demon faces are illuminated as they sparkle and appear like tiny specs of gold glitter…

"You got de' money?" Scratch demands.

Said with a thick west-Indian accent.

"Yeah, I got it," Michael responds.

He takes the wad of cash Buns had spotted him from his pocket and hands it over.

"So, what is your wish? Scratch demands. "You having trouble wid your boss, right?"

"Ummm…Yeah… So, dis' fucking prick at my job is always messing with me for no reason. He picks on me, yells at me, insults me, he even put his hands on me, and pushed me… and nobody's doing anything to stop it… I'm sick of it," Michael says. "I feel like he is trying to destroy me or something. I'm struggling with this. I feel anxious and irritable about it. I can't really focus, and all I think about – is destroying him, because of his outlandish behavior, and the way he constantly disrespects me. I feel like I have no choice – I have to defend myself.

I *wish* that he would just leave me the fuck alone and go away!" Michael says.

Scratch responds rather plainly, "Okay. I take care of it. You have something of his?"

Michael pulls out the comb and gives it to scratch. Scratch takes it, walks over to a shelf against the wall, tears off a piece of paper from a notebook, and grabs a pencil. He gives the paper and pencil to Michael. "Write his name down, on this piece of paper."

Michael does so, and Scratch presents yet another command.

"Take off your shoes."

Michael hands Scratch the paper and then takes off his shoes. Scratch puts the paper on the floor and makes Michael stand on it. He closes his eyes and whispers an incantation, then takes a paintbrush in a mop bucket with copious amounts of foul-smelling liquid, which looks like blood. Scratch washes the blood on Michael's feet and mumbles a repetitive chant in patois. He opens a piece of bloody wax paper with a cow's tongue inside; he pulls hair strands from the comb and puts them on the cow tongue, then pounds six rusty nails into it, re-wraps the paper, and ties up the tongue with a rope, and lights it on fire, but then blows it out shortly after that. He then takes Michael's shoes and uses white chalk to draw strange symbols on the bottom underside of the shoes.

Finally, he takes the wooden wish box with the illuminated eyes on it and puts the now bloody piece of paper with the name on it into the box and the remaining hair strands from the comb.

He grabs Michael's hand, places it on the box, whispers more chants, and forcibly presses Michael's hand down onto a small sharp spike at the top of the box that Michael had not noticed before. Blood spurts out of the gash in Michael's palm into the box via small funnels inside the small spike. The demon within the box exits as a wisp of thick, black ectoplasm, along with an evil-looking, demonic face embedded within flaming embers, and unnoticed by Michael circles around behind him and swiftly flies into Michael's back, temporarily disorienting him, and his eyes momentarily turn completely black, then revert to normal.

"What the hell… Did you just feel that? What the fuck just happened? I feel strange…and what did you do, that box cut my hand…"

Looking down at his now excessively bleeding palm… Michael grabs a dirty rag from a nearby side table and wraps his bleeding hand.

"De' contract is struck! As you wished, your enemy is now bound, and is trapped under your feet… I have silenced his tongue against you…and you are protected. He will leave you alone. Now, de' final piece – with your blood you are now bound to dis wish box! Take it – it belongs to you now," Scratch states cryptically, handing him the wish box, which he bled into.

"But you will need to satisfy the spirit in the box and put something that belongs to the sacrificed inside the box as your offering to the dark lord," Scratch adds.

"What dark lord, and what sacrifice? What are you talking about? I'm not sacrificing anything, I just want my boss to stop messing with me that's all," Michael corrects.

Scratch ignores the comment and continues.

Scratch asserts, "I told you, your boss will stop bothering you, as you wished. But, the wish box will also provide you with other far more generous gifts... I look at you, look in your eyes, and I can see that your job is very important to you eh... You are ambitious... You want to rise to the top of your company... You secretly lust for the money and power that has escaped you all your life. Well, the spirit of the box will grant you all of this - *your deepest innermost wishes and dreams, spoken and unspoken.* You will immediately prosper greatly in everything you desire at your job, promotion, women, everything you want... and in return, all you have to do is simply make an offering, by putting something that belongs to the one sacrificed into the box," Scratch states.

The room is spinning as Michael exhibits more signs of dizziness and disorientation — making up feel like down, and down feel like up.

"You said sacrifice, but you just mean — that I just have put something that belongs to my boss in the box every day, like his pen, or his comb or something like that right?" Michael asks for further clarification.

Scratch explains, "What you put in the box is an offering and that can be anything that belongs to the one sacrificed... but it won't just be something from your boss..."

"I told you, I don't want to hear about no sacrifice. All I want is for my boss get off my back...," Michael demands.

"You will come to understand everything in due time... Sometime de demon mark you even before you get mark for real...Sometimes de' demon marks you in your dreams...," Scratch says with a broad, wicked smile.

With those words, Michael now remembers where he had seen Scratch before... it was from his recurring dream where he is chasing his father down an abandoned street. Scratch was the cloaked man/entity with a scratch or scar on the right side of his face that appeared to him in the dream and offered him the gold coins and the face of a demon... Michael is now starting to become even more dizzy and disoriented.

"You! It was you...You've been in my dreams... I've seen you in my dreams... but how did you..."

"Listen to me b'woy... Wid' dis wish box, if you miss even one day, of not giving the spirit something back, or leaving de' wish box open without submitting a sacrifice or putting something inside the box from someone sacrificed... bad things will happen...," Scratch states.

"What they are you talking about?" says Michael.

Michael staggers forward, and the room starts swirling. He trips and falls forward but is caught by Scratch...his eyes turn black again for a brief moment but then turn back to normal, and he stumbles again... Michael is completely disoriented now, and Scratch's voice sounds heavily distorted, and like it is coming from inside a tunnel, and the room continues spinning...

"De' demon has taken full root," Scratch says, now with an even wider evil grin on his face.

"Wha...what did you do to me? What's happening?"

Michael hears Scratch's voice, but the sound is muffled and appears to be coming from far away. He can barely listen to what is being said.

"You will achieve money, favor, and fortune, and in exchange, you will be transformed into a demon. You will be able to revert back to human form, but to do so, you must eat human flesh. This will only stop the transformation for a time, but then you will eventually turn again, becoming the demon, in a cycle that will end with your soul. Once you kill and feed off the flesh of six people, you will then become a demon forever! Feed de' box or you will not be able to control the unending hunger for flesh…which will eventually devour your soul." Scratch proclaims.

Michael is still highly dizzy and gradually regains his senses, but Scratch suddenly appears aggressively annoyed.

"Time for you to go! I have told you everything you need to know! You have been given exactly what you came here for! Remember, make a sacrifice, and give an offering belonging to the sacrificed back to de' box… and never open the box without putting something inside de' box... This is your contract, bound by your blood!" Scratch emphasized.

Scratch grabs him by the arm, leads him to the front door, and pushes him out. Michael stands outside the door, staring blankly in the darkness, unsure what just happened. He looks down at the wish box in his hand, walks down the hallway, up the stairs, and exits the building, where he meets up with Buns, who has been waiting. Buns looks at him, then at the box Michael clutches under his arm, and then back to Michael, who stares blankly, unsure of exactly what has just happened...

11 UNICORN UNVEILED

The sun is still rising on the Big Apple, but Michael is already at his desk – it's 7:00 a.m. The office is still and quiet, as hardly anyone is in. He does notice that Betancourt's door is closed, and the light is on, indicating that he is there, but he does not come out. Michael places the wooden wish box on his desk and stares at it blankly for some time… Then he moves it over to the corner of his desk. His stomach makes a loud groaning and gurgling sound, which startles him, but he ignores it… The entire morning, Michael keeps expecting Betancourt to come out and berate and attack him, but there is no sign of him… 8:45 a.m. comes, and it's time for the account meeting. Finally, Betancourt exits his office and heads to the conference room. Other employees, including Michael, file in, and Mr. Freeman arrives as always 5 minutes before to start the meeting promptly at 9:00 a.m.

The main conference room is where the creative and account teams assemble to meet with Mr. Freeman, who is chairing the meeting. Roger comes from money – old money. His father made his fortune back in the forties in real estate. Allegedly acquired his first apartment building in a card game in the old neighborhood, and then built himself up from there. His father always wanted Roger to eventually join the family business. Although he tried it for a time after graduating from college, he soon found that he could neither tolerate working with his father for long hours nor even minutes, and he basically decided to utilize the business degree he earned and pursue his own fortune. Roger felt that having to sometimes bang on doors looking for late rent or other deadbeat situations was beneath him. He particularly despised going to the Bronx to get owed rent from tenants in the buildings they owned. His distaste for real estate management aside, he always had a creative streak in him, and eventually, after leaving his father's real estate empire, he got a job at one of the larger advertising agencies in New York, where he worked for several years, making his way to the top. His father died shortly after, leaving his real estate empire without a leader. His father had done quite well for himself and owned multiple properties, mostly tenant rental buildings within The Bronx, Brooklyn, and one prime piece of real estate in Manhattan. So, Roger sold his father's company and cashed out as a millionaire. However, smartly retained the crown jewel of his father's empire on East Third Avenue, Manhattan. Roger redid the building with external and internal gold fixtures, alluding to the opulence and wealth he intended to surround himself with. The gold finishes make the building look exotic and expensive but also loud and gaudy at the same time. Roger established his own agency in that building and called it Bold Advertising, adorning the building with the now iconic "B" logo high atop the building. Bold grew from originally being just on the 15th floor to eventually growing and taking over floors 15 through 32, and construction on a 33rd floor was slated to come online in two years. The mail room for Bold Advertising was eventually moved to the basement floor, and floors 1-14 were all rented out to other companies. So, despite not being interested in real estate initially, ultimately, to some degree, Roger still ended up as somebody's landlord. It was a wild ride for the business tycoon when he was first starting out, as he used his money and connections within the industry to plunder some of his competitors' top talent and employees. Like its founder, Bold Advertising became known for being fiercely competitive, unconventional, and an innovative advertising agency, garnering large clients and accounts from very early on. Although the company was a smaller boutique agency, Roger ran it like one of the big top agencies, with an enforceable dress code and a list of policies and rules a mile long. He was always big on optics and infused and developed a culture within the company where everyone looked like money. H.R. was instructed to hire only attractive, good-looking people with high I.Q.s and provable high academic rankings out of college. The company became known as the place where all the pretty people worked. All the men dressed in suits, and the women never wore pants. By his design, Roger set the tone for the misogynistic, sexist, and biased undertones that would continue to dog the company for years to come and shape its culture. From the company's inception, Roger was never big on hiring minorities, at least not in the company's core operations. He never says anything bad about race, but is always aloof around people who don't look like him. When interacting with people of another racial background, he is uncomfortable and conducts himself with a rigid, and unmistakable air of superiority. So, while he never says or does anything outwardly racist, by choice he generally only associates or chooses to do business with people that look like him. Until recently, he lived a life completely devoid of people of color, except for those few who served him, such as his driver, maids, etc. His head of security, Mr. Charleswell, started as his driver before being allowed to work within the company. The country clubs and places he vacationed were too exclusive and expensive for anyone of color to get into, even if they could afford it. Eventually, because of affirmative action rules and the cultural changes in time, he was, if not reluctantly, forced to hire more minorities, which he promptly placed in the mailroom, security, or the cleaning staff. However, because he always had an eye for beautiful women, the few women of color were hired only because they served as eye candy for him. Roger's preference was always for attractive model-type blondes. However, he would not turn up an opportunity to bed a beautiful woman of any color. In fact, it was always alleged that Roger and Jessica Reyes had an affair when she was first hired, but it was never proven, and she later married a prominent African-American attorney and became Mrs. Jessica Reyes-Powell. After that, the rumors, for the most part, went away. Roger's wife was a French, former runway model named Amiel. However, their marriage was short-lived, and the eventual divorce was always obvious due to Roger's wandering eye and philandering ways. Although older, the silver fox, as he is called by some of his competitors because of his white head of hair today, still runs his company with an iron hand. In his heady youth, he had a huge sexual appetite, which continues to this day, with the help of his ED treatment pills. Roger knew that large amounts of money always serve as a potent aphrodisiac to attract women, and he used that approach to serve his desires.

Roger and Amiel separated amicably, with her getting a fair sum of money in the settlement, but what Roger treasured the most coming out of the union was his only child, his daughter Tiffany, whom he adores. Roger has Tiffany interning at the company, mostly because he wants to be closer to his daughter. He feels guilty that for most of her young life, when she was growing up, he was never around, either working, traveling, or sleeping around, and so now that she is eighteen and basically an adult, he wants to make up for that last time. He marvels at how much she looks like her mother, blonde hair and physique. As he looks at her out of the corner of his eye, he can't help but feel so proud of her – his one and only daughter.

Roger sits at the edge of his chair to emphasize his point, "So, I recognize that we are on a bit of a tight schedule, but we're here to brainstorm," He says. "We've got to get some concrete ideas on the table. I received some email concept submissions yesterday, but only from the account team… I did not receive any from the creative team. He glances over at Jessica, who avoids his stare and continues looking down at her notes and scribbling… So, I will assume that both teams collaborated on this joint submission. Anyway, the ideas I received…. They weren't half bad, I think. He puts the list up on the screen for the team to see. I will draw your attention to slogan #5: "Nagasaki is the bomb!" Roger states.

"Dirk raises his hand, "Yeah that was mine… I umm…," Roger cuts him off before he can continue.

"Yeah, I actually saw that as way too edgy and could border on or be perceived as an insult to our Japanese clients, for obvious reasons…," Roger states. "So, it might be a good idea to stay away from themes like that…." he says, "However, there is one item that I needed further clarification on. He puts the list he received from Dirk back up on the screen. One of the things on the list that appeared to be quite unusual was item #10, which simply says, "Drip."… Dirk, do you want to explain exactly what this is? "Was that a typo or just an incomplete thought?" Roger asks.

Sensing that Freeman would go negative again and not wishing to further taint himself, Dirk punted and took a different approach…

"Well, I ummm… uhhh… See that one wasn't exactly mine, and I actually didn't even want to include it… that concept was actually the only contribution coming from our new Assistant Trainee – Michael Hill." Dirk smiles slyly as the spotlight is now placed on Michael. Dirk figures this is a way to throw Michael under the bus and embarrass the young man. Mr. Freeman looks at him and smiles, non-verbally indicating that Michael has the floor. Michael stands up and goes to the front of the room. He pauses and then starts to speak in a straightforward and controlled manner…

"Well sir, I was trying to go for a more urban niche appeal approach for this client, than what they have traditionally done in their marketing. Our research shows that the automotive category is huge, with consumers spending over ninety billion dollars on automotive accessories alone, including custom tires and accessories. Of course, this category is primarily dominated by men. Many of these consumers are high-end consumers, owners of luxury or performance-made automobiles, but there is also a subset of minority consumers in our urban centers who are also very much interested in having a fly ride," Michael explains. Everyone in the room is focused on Michael, listening intently to every word he says.

"So, I am proposing that we target that under-tapped market by devising a campaign that speaks to that audience and brings them together with the general market consumers under the one thing they both want – performance… To do so, we will capitalize on a popular current urban term and marry that popular hip term to our client's product to promote the product as being new, hip, and popular. The socially popular word Drip means to have swagger. It means you're hot, you're cool. You're on point… So, going with that concept, our ad will open with the definition of the word "Drip" along with a banging hip-hop beat, then cut to a leaking water faucet that is dripping, but instead of dripping water, it is dripping rubber, which when it hits the ground form into a Nagasaki Tire, the verbiage on the screen will say – Cover your rims in style! When performance matters – Choose Nagasaki Tires – The Ultimate Drip for Your Whip!" and then fade to black," Michael concludes.

Dirk is in complete disbelief at what he has just heard. He never dreamed Michael was this articulate and this familiar with the pitch process. The room is still and quiet; no one moves, and no sound is heard… Mr. Freeman sits stoically, absolutely still, looking directly at Michael. Finally, Mr. Freeman yells out with a huge smile.

"I love it! I absolutely love it! This is a great concept, its hip, it's urban, it's fresh, and definitely fits our company's brand with regards to producing campaigns which are irreverent, current, and in touch with the market and consumers reflected in a next level brand integration and recognition approach. These are the principles and campaigns that Bold Advertising was founded on, and is known for," Roger proclaims almost giddy.

Everyone in the room begins clapping and looks directly at Michael, beaming with smiles. Everyone except Dirk Betancourt.

"My boy, you're a natural genius! I want work on all other projects stopped, immediately! We'll use three of the other more traditional concepts as back-ups, but I want to lead and go full speed ahead with our pitch utilizing this specific concept! I want… what's your name again, son?"

"Michael, sir…Michael Hill," says Michael. Shaking Mr. Freeman's offered hand vigorously.

"Well, Michael Hill, I want you working directly with Jessica and her team to quickly ramp up and produce a spot and related creative to pitch the Nagasaki executives."

"Are you fucking kidding me! He's a junior associate, he doesn't know his ass from a hole in the ground!" Screams Dirk. "Michael reports to me, so as V.P. of the Account team, I should be handling the interface between the account side and the creative team, not some kid…"

Roger looks at him sternly, "I'm sorry, but didn't you just tell me that it was his idea?"

"Well, yes… But team protocol dictates that I as V.P. head up all efforts… Especially something as big as this account," Dirk explains.

Roger counters, "I don't give a damn about protocol! I set the protocol here, and I care more about profit! And my gut tells me that I can make a profit with this young man's concept! All I know is that this young man came up with a concept that is impressive – and has the potential to knock the socks off this client! That's what I care about! That's what matters – landing this lucrative account! You didn't come up with any ideas for this pitch, did you? Actually, remind me again, what is the last account that you landed anyway? Or, are you just resting on what you've done in the past, to carry you through…? You know the rules

– it's never personal, it's what have you done for me lately right Dirk...," looking at him directly into his eyes.

Dirk is fuming and yells, "Well, then I quit!" he exclaims.

"Then quit!" Roger fires back. "Tell me what part of what I just said that you didn't understand... I believe that I made my wishes absolutely clear, and that's all! Meeting adjourned!" Roger asserts.

Roger gets up and leaves the conference room followed by Maria, the receptionist from the 31st floor acting as Roger's assistant, along with his daughter, Tiffany. The room erupts into loud conversation back and forth, with other team members congratulating Michael, patting him on the back, and all talking with him at once. Michael smiles and is overwhelmed by all of the attention and feedback. Dirk Betancourt stares in disbelief, and slowly, his disbelief turns to a silent rage, and he storms out of the room.

Over the next few days, Michael is working closely with Jessica and the creative team and putting together the storyboards and the creative spots for the Nagasaki executives. They are all smiling and working in sync in the conference room.

Dirk Betancourt is no longer actively participating in the process and appears lost and disoriented. He walks by outside the conference room, looking in, and when he looks at Michael, his face becomes tight, red, and angry.

Everything around the office is wholly focused on the Nagasaki account. So, one day, Jimmy is in the copy room making copies for the presentation and accidentally drops some files on the floor. He bends down to retrieve them but then sees some photocopies under the copier; he pulls them out and sees the graphic images of Dirk and Tiffany. He is disgusted and clutches the photos angrily and in disbelief as his feelings for Tiffany are wholly crushed by the graphic images he sees.

Michael is sitting at his desk. On his computer, he clicks on Google, enters "Voodoo Caribbean Black Magic" into the search engine, and several listings appear. He clicks on the first one, "Caribbean Occult and Black Magic," and begins reading. The search engine shows, "The practice of voodoo is the belief that one can use certain spirits or supernatural agents to harm the living, or to call them off from such mischief." He comes to a section listed "Enchantments & Charms from the Eastern Caribbean," where he briefly views a listing for *"Obeah," "Sweat Rice,"* and other associated terminology and illustrated depictions.

He continues and goes to the section listed "sorcery & definitions." He finds the word "voodoo – a sorcery practiced especially in the Caribbean." He also sees the words *"jumbie"* and *"demon"* – an evil spirit or devil, especially one thought to possess a person." He continues and finds a listing for *"Wish box"* – a device housing a demon tied to a living person's soul and changing the person into a monster, killing and consuming human flesh.

The cursed person will be transformed into a demon, and to revert back and maintain human form, he must kill and consume human flesh, taking artifacts from his victims and placing them as an offering into the wish box. The artifacts forever tie the souls of the victims to hell. After the killing and cannibalization of six victims, the cursed individual will permanently become a demon on earth. Those souls of the victims killed become occupants of hell, and their place is taken by demons who enter this earthly plane and occupy a wish box in a never-ending cycle where the metaphysical becomes physical. So, hell receives a new pipeline providing an influx of new souls, and conversely, demons from hell are transported to earth to create a new era of hell on earth.

The demons are summoned to this world using "The Book of The Dead" to communicate with Congo Savanne, an evil Voodoo deity and cannibalistic demon, which demands cannibalism on the part of those it possesses.. Persons using the book can create a portal on a wall to enable the demons to cross over from hell into the wish box and then enter or possess a human host as a wisp of thick, black ectoplasm.

He sees graphic imagery showing how unsuspecting victims are lured to the box by the lust for riches, power, and the pleasures of the flesh. He reads further that the wish box in some Caribbean nations is sometimes referred to as a wish box or a glitter box because the demonic eyes on the demonic faces on the box appear like specs of gold glitter when there is a sinister presence within the box. Once it is activated, it helps to make the box appear alluring to unsuspecting victims. His final entry reads, "The owner of the wish box is cursed for life…"

He sees additional ancient evil and bizarre images etched into the walls of caves showing the wish box, including graphic scenes depicting owners and their boxes, with black gashes in their palms. A footnote indicates that the black magic of voodoo interferes with electrical fields and that a new strain of evil voodoo is being fused with Satanism. He then sees an image of Congo Savanne. The text under the image of the demon reads, "The cursed individual and owner of the wish box, after eating the flesh of six victims, will be permanently stuck in demon form and will no longer be able to become human again." At that point, Michael closes the search engine and is overcome by emotion as he more clearly remembers what Scratch told him about transformation, which he has seen and confirmed word for word on the internet. He is overcome with grief and tears, looking away as he is now fully aware of what will happen to him and, more importantly, what the curse will make him do…

The days go by quickly, leading up to D-Day – the pitch to the Nagasaki executives. Dirk appears to be falling off and does not even look like himself. He is unshaven and has grown a full beard, and although in a business suit, he is tieless; he does not look like his usual self and is sitting towards the end of the conference room table.

The executives from Nagasaki Tires walk in, and all Asian executives wearing expensive business suits are led in by the receptionist from the 31st floor, Maria. Maria and Mona usher the executives into the room and have them all sit on one side of the table. The executives from Bold Advertising are already in the room. Roger Freeman stands, as do all his team, to greet team Nagasaki. Roger takes the lead in shaking hands; he is flanked by V.P. of creative, Jessica Reyes-Powell, and seated next to her is Michael, and other creative team members.

As people are still mulling around, Roger notices Dirk sitting in the corner, looking pale and distracted, so Roger walks over to him.

"Dirk, what the hell happened to you? You look like shit... Are you alright?" Roger asks.

"Yeah... No... I mean, I haven't really been feeling well lately.... I don't know... I'm not myself, I'm not sleeping, and my tongue hurts every time I try to speak," Dirk explains, then starts laughing uncontrollably. People around them turn around and give him dirty looks, which they both notice. Dirk starts whispering, "Strange things are happening man... I mean, sometimes I feel like I'm losing my fucking mind! Know what I'm saying... The other day, I swore someone went into my office, but didn't take a damned thing except for my comb... I mean, can you believe that... why would anyone do that, right? I don't feel like doing anything except being locked up in my house or office, which isn't like me... I constantly feel run down, tired, and anxious all at the same time... and you want to know the craziest part of it – I keep feeling claustrophobic like I'm in a box that I can't get out of... I mean, is that completely crazy or what?" he blurts out.

Dirk is both laughing and crying at the same time, appearing completely unhinged.

"My God, man, you really need to see someone… And all this because I took the Nagasaki account away from you? Look, take some time off, take a vacation or something, but get yourself together!"

"Yeah, yeah, of course I'll be alright… I just need some… some time… that's all, just… I…," Dirk continues on, but Roger has already wholly disengaged from the conversation and moved on to start the meeting…

Roger begins, "… And so, gentlemen, we want to warmly welcome you to Bold Advertising. We feel that Bold can help to market your company's premium tires here in North America, by using a niche marketing approach, by appealing to consumers with performance-based vehicles. Now, I will turn it over to the lead account representative on your account – Mr. Michael Hill, who will make our pitch," Roger says.

"Thank you, Roger… Gentlemen, Nagasaki is a premium brand representing quality, luxury, and performance. You have established yourselves overseas as a leading automotive brand, and we at Bold Advertising would like to assist you in continuing your winning ways here in the American Market.

Our team comprises industry leaders with over one hundred years of solid marketing, account management, and creative experience. So, we not only know the market, but we directly research, track, and incorporate consumer trends into all of our successful campaigns, many of which have garnered critical acclaim and awards. We want to bring our know-how and expertise to make Nagasaki the number-one tire brand in America! We have some marketing proofs and concepts to demonstrate our strategy and approach! Susan, could you hit the lights, please? Ladies and Gentlemen, prepare to experience the Nagasaki Drip!" Michael proclaims.

The executives watch the slick and stylized marketing campaign and associated supporting social media and print materials utilizing the "Nagasaki Drip" concept. After the campaign, the Nagasaki executives are quiet, serious, and say nothing.

Michael walks up to the executives, "Gentlemen, we would really like the opportunity to work with your company, and help take your business to the next level financially here in the States… and make us all a whole lot of money… What do you say?" Michael extends his hand to the lead businessman.

There is a long pause… The businessmen look at each other and nod to each other, conferring non-verbally, then…

"We love it! We love this concept! We want your agency to represent us!"

The men excitedly shake hands, and the Bold Advertising team opens multiple chilled bottles of Veuve Clicquot. Employees inside the conference room and within the entire floor give thunderous applause, and the mood is festive and joyous. Michael is celebrated as a hero, as a star, and for the first time in a very long time, Michael feels very much wanted and appreciated, despite the intense gravity of the horror that he now knows lies deep within him.

12 DREAMING

After the success of closing the account, the next few days are a blur. Additionally, Michael finds that he has been fatigued and always starving as of late. No matter how much he eats, he still does not get full and never feels satisfied.

It's late at night, and Michael is in bed watching TV. He flips channels and lands on Cartoon Network, showing a vintage black and white animated Disney cartoon titled *"Hell's Bells."* He watches for a bit but eventually nods off to sleep, and instead of watching TV, the TV is now watching him. He begins having a very vivid dream. Outside of his dream, his eyelids are rapidly moving in REM sleep. Within his dream, the colors he sees are over-saturated and flashy, with lots of reds and psychedelic bright colors.

In the dream, he feels like he is outside of his own body and viewing a scene from a movie. He sees the interior of a manhole and sees stagnant water filled with large amounts of human waste. He thinks the dream feels so real that he can literally smell the noxious sulfur stench of the brackish wastewater. Except for several floating and moving pieces of fecal matter on the surface, the murky water is otherwise still until suddenly the water begins bubbling, and the head of a demon slowly rises from below the water. The demon extends its clawed hand to a nearby ladder and begins to gradually climb up the ladder. The large black demon has an angry, and evil looking face, with piercing blood-red eyes. Jutting out of the back of the demon's elongated skull is a single large ram's horn, which comes to a sharp curved point at the top of its right shoulder. The demon's body is an emaciated, skeleton-like torso with long muscular arms and legs.. The demon stealthily climbs the sewer ladder, with the brackish water dripping from its body, its blood-red eyes illuminating the dark. The monster slowly pushes open the storm drain cover and emerges within a tunnel of the train tracks of the NYC subway. The demon runs on four legs through the tunnel to the nearby platform and crawls onto the back section of the crowded forum. The lights start blinking wildly on the platform, and people begin to cover their noses when they smell an incredibly foul odor. People then see the demon and immediately start screaming and running away from it. The demon initially continues attacking and walking on all four legs, but then stands upright, is bipedal, and begins running on two legs, hissing, scratching, and biting several people on the subway platform. The demon literally scratches the face of the man with claws so sharp that they slice his face off, horribly disfiguring him for life; luckily, a medical attendant near him can quickly begin to render critical aid to stop the bleeding and save the man's life.

The bestial-looking demon roars and displays several rows of sharp, jagged teeth, protruding from its mouths, The demon displays its weaponry to the fleeing crowds, which includes one sharp and elongated index claw amidst its other digits. The demon is built like an apex predator – built to kill. A man begins running away, but the demon lands on him and starts aggressively chasing him; the man jumps down on the train tracks and begins running into the tunnel, and the demon pursues. The man is screaming and throws his briefcase at the demon, but it still keeps coming. The demon leaps into the air in front of the man and, standing before him, begins scratching his stomach out with both claws at rapid speeds, gutting and disemboweling the man as he stands haplessly watching and shaking as he is gutted. The demon then savagely bites and clamps down on the man's throat, ripping it out. After the man dies, the demon grabs the man's wallet, an artifact of *its first victim*.

A transit cop following the activity onto the track sees the demon savaging the man and fires several rounds directly into the demon. The demon looks back and snarls at the cop, and then chases him. The cop turns around and dashes back to the platform, with the demon in pursuit and eventually catching him. As soon as he is about to make it back up on the platform, the demon punches his hand through the cop's chest from the back, extracting his heart, pulling it out his back, placing it into his mouth, and eating it. The cop limply falls to the ground, the demon snatches the officer's badge from his shirt as its chosen artifact, and then grabs the cop's limp body, placing the body of *its second victim* on its shoulder, and jumps up onto the platform.

A train is now entering the station, heavily applying the brakes and partially derailing. The demon leaps back onto the platform, carrying the lifeless carcass and the artifacts. People are scattering in all directions, with the demon snarling at them and running on all four legs, up the stairs from the train platform, up to the upper level where the turnstiles are, and then up the stairs and out on to the street, causing massive car accidents and related explosions, as the demon runs in the traffic for several blocks. Several police cruisers eventually intercept the demon, with police officers immediately exiting the creature and shooting it at point-blank range – with absolutely no effect. The demon hisses at them and retreats in the opposite direction, running on all fours, eventually running into a darkened alley, opening a manhole cover, and going down into the sewer. Finally, the demon emerges from a manhole directly in a dark alley behind Michael's building. The demon takes the body and the artifacts, scales the rear building wall, and slithers into his open apartment window, carrying the officer's limp body.

In his apartment, Michael has now partially reverted back to human. He is in a corner of the apartment and has a depraved and evil look on his face. He is extremely pale, with black circles underneath his eyes. His face is bloody, and he is savagely eating the remains of the police officer's ribs. His eyes have reverted from demonic red to lifeless black.

He continues to slowly revert back to human and regains control. His eyes return to normal; he is naked, awash with sweat… His window is open, and next to his bed, on a nightstand, is the wish box, and inside it is a bloody wallet and the officer's bloody badge… The wish box then automatically shuts. Michael is horrified and repulsed as he comes to his senses and is in immediate shock as he realizes that none of this was a dream – it was all real…

13 MOVING ON UP

Roger has three television screens in his office, which are side by side. The monitor on the left is tuned to CNBC for stocks and financial information. The one on the right is tuned to Fox News. The tv in the middle is tuned to NY1 for local news; this screen is where the volume is turned on.

The NY1 anchor exclaims, "Our round-the-clock coverage continues, with news of the gruesome multiple killings and attacks last night on the Brooklyn IRT #2 subway line. Eyewitnesses on the scene have provided conflicting reports, including smelling some type of foul odor, then reported seeing either a large, deformed man or some kind of large, wild animal savagely attack, maim, and kill several people within the subway, including a decorated NYPD officer, whose being dubbed a hero for helping to fight the killer, but whose body has not yet been found.

A massive search for the missing police officer, whose name has not yet been released to the public, has been launched within the subway tunnels. Anonymous sources within the NYPD told NY1 that mysteriously, all video cameras within that area of the subway station had some type of electrical glitch and did not capture any footage of the killings…" the anchor concludes.

Roger isn't paying attention to the news as he is participating in a video conference call at his desk. Buns comes down the aisle pushing his mail cart and stops in front of Roger's office, where Maria stands before the door. He smiles generously at her, but she turns her face away rudely.

Buns hands Maria several letters and packages. Maria then takes the mail into Roger's office and places it on the desk. Roger begins to open his mail as he is talking. He opens several envelopes, but then comes to a sizeable interoffice envelope with his name on it and the words Open Me written in bright red lipstick. When he opens it, it is the Xerox pictures of Tiffany having sex with Dirk, and written in bright red lipstick are the words, "Is this your innocent angel?"

"What the hell!!! Maria, get Dirk Betancourt down here right NOW!!!," yells Roger as he immediately drops from the conference call.

Maria makes the call immediately and informs Dirk that he needs to come to Roger's office directly, which he does. As he exits the elevator on Roger's floor, he can't imagine what would be so crucial that Roger needs to see him immediately. He walks past Maria's desk and walks into Roger's office.

"Hi, Roger. You wanted to see me?" says Dirk.

"No, I actually really don't want to see you! Shut the fucking door!" he yells.

Roger pitches the envelope with color photocopies across the desk before Dirk. Dirk is stunned, immediately recognizes the images, and looks away ashamed, as he closes the door and sits down.

"Oh my God, Roger… Look I'm sorry… I didn't mean for that to happen…," Dirk confesses.

"You didn't mean it!" You didn't mean it? What the hell did you mean? Roger asks.

"Look… Tiffany and I… one thing led to another, and we had a romantic encounter and…"

"Is that what you call it? A romantic encounter – with my daughter, on top of a fucking copy machine no less?"

Becoming frustrated, Dirk raises his voice, "Look, I'm sorry… things got out of hand… I thought I had cleaned up all the photocopies… I must have missed some, and someone… obviously found them and sent them to you, to get back at me, and I think I know who that is…"

"No, you're not sorry you did it – you're just sorry you got caught! Listen asshole! I turned a blind eye and tolerated all of your drug use, with your little saber-tooth drug club within my company – think I didn't know about all of that? All your harassment and abuse of female employees – all of your bullshit! And I left you alone, just so long as you keep bringing in the money - and in return, this is how you repay me? By taking advantage of my little girl? Let me ask you something; from the looks of both of you, did you give my little girl drugs?

Dirk looks away and avoids eye contact.

"I asked you a fucking question! You fucked my daughter, and did you give my little girl drugs? Look at me, look at me! Did you give her drugs?"

Dirk feels trapped and doesn't know how to respond, "… Look, we both took a hit…but it was nothing."

"You fucking piece of shit! You crossed the line! You completely crossed the fucking line this time! You knew that she was off-limits! This is my daughter! She's a child, dammit!"

"Roger, please. Look, I'm sorry…," Dirk pleads.

"You're fired!!! I want your ass out of my sight! The only reason I'm not turning you over to the authorities and pressing charges against you is because, unfortunately, you are still involved in several of the projects that we already have in process. So, I'll give you a couple of days to turn over your accounts, and once that's done, I want you out of here. I never want to see you again and stay the hell away from my daughter! Now get the fuck out of my office!"

Dirk quickly exits the office, fleeing from Roger's palpable wrath.

The sun has long since set across the city that never sleeps. It is raining heavily again in Brooklyn, and Michael is staring at the cathedral's front door for a long time. Tears run down his face as he stares blankly at the cathedral doors. Michael is conflicted and confused. He grew up in a deeply religious household and, as a result, has decided to come to the church for help to stop this insidious and evil curse. Already, he can clearly see the benefits of the curse working – Betancourt has backed off of him, and just as Scratch said, he's already quickly advancing in wealth and status within the company – but at what cost? Michael is receiving everything promised to him, but he's already killed two people to maintain everything he has received thus far, and will have to kill others to achieve more. After six kills, what happens then…? So, everything Scratch told him and everything he read on those black magic websites has come true. But now that he's actually done it – killed and eaten people, how can he possibly go on like this, literally killing his way to success… But is it worth all this just for a career, money, and status?

Finally, he musters up the courage to come out of the pouring rain, walk up to the door, and walk inside. However, as soon as he walks inside in direct response to stepping on holy ground, the bones in his legs snap and crack, and he falls to the floor, writhing in pain. Desperate not to be stopped, he begins dragging himself forward into the church. His eyes are now entirely black. The church is empty except for the Priest, who is up at the altar putting out the candles on the altar. He turns around to see Michael dragging himself, but it does not immediately register with him what he is seeing.

"I'm sorry my son, but if you're here for our last service for the evening, I'm afraid you've already missed it… I know that all of this rain threw some people's schedule off, but you can come always, come back tomorrow," says Father Mulligan with a smile. "I was just about to lock up…"

Michael continues dragging his legs as he advances forward in the church; he comes up to a point where a crucifix is mounted on a staff at the front of the center aisle. He looks up at the cross and roars defiantly at the cross, and suddenly, the cross is engulfed in flames. Michael begins rapidly transforming into a demon, then rapidly changing back to human form. He can't fully transform and is caught in an endless repetitious transformation loop because he is on Holy ground. Father Mulligan now clearly sees and realizes this is no ordinary church attendee.

"Get out! Get out of the house of the Lord, unclean creature! You don't belong here! I rebuke you in the name of the most high, Jesus Christ! Go back to hell where you belong!" says the priest commandingly.

"No… wait! You don't understand, help me… I came for help…"

An earthquake suddenly occurs within the church, knocking the priest to the ground. However, from the floor, he continues to rebuke the demon.

"Get back into the pit of hell that spawned you, demon! You have no power here, and you have no right to be here in the house of the Lord! You will obey every command in Jesus' name!"

The priest does not hear Michael's continued call for help. The priest continues with his powerful and strong rebukes. He is holding the holy bible and begins speaking in Latin. Michael starts writhing in pain and frothing at the mouth as the priest says, almost to the point of passing out.

Father Mulligan is a renowned exorcist who happens to be serving and hiding at this cathedral in Brooklyn. Seeing this vile hell spawn in his church dredges him with painful memories. It's been six years since he had been transferred to the parish, after the incident in South Florida. A young girl had been reported to have been possessed, and Father Mulligan was dispatched by the Church to investigate the situation. In fact, within just six weeks of the first reported possession of the young girl, a sudden and unexplained rash of several other demonic possessions also began happening and being reported within that area. Father Mulligan had planned to deal with the young girl first and then address the others that had seemingly popped as a cluster not far from the first girl's physical location. The girl showed all the marked signs of possession, including pain and aversion to prayers and religious holy symbols, pronounced activity at 3:00 a.m., and mysterious, unexplained three-clawed scratches on her back and arms.

After the standard tests that the church requires, Father Mulligan concluded that the girl was possessed. One of the things that was highly troubling about this particular case was the girl's seemingly uncontrollable, self-mutilation, and cannibalistic tendencies; even though she had been bound and tied to her bed, she would break free and bite and consume huge chunks out of her own arms and legs, and would also try to bite others. Her possession was nothing he had ever encountered before, as the demon inside her was extraordinarily violent and, despite a long and protracted battle, would not give the priest its name so that it could be driven out.

The priest later discovered that there was a sect of demon worshipers, led by a powerful voodoo priest, who were practicing an offshoot of satanic worship mixed with voodoo, which involved an evil voodoo entity called Congo Savanne, which proved to be very powerful and robust and was behind the possessions within the area. In the end, the priest was victorious and eventually vanquished the evil spirit, but it was at a high cost because soon after, the young girl died due to the rigorous exorcism that the priest had to do to drive the evil spirit out. Once she died, the other cases of possessions seemed to suddenly stop, and those who were previously possessed could no longer be found or located.

The young girl who died was the daughter of a powerful elected official, and in his grief and sadness, he began a very public quest and legal onslaught against the priest and the church over the death of his daughter. He blamed the church and Father Mulligan for the death of his daughter, although he was the one who contacted the church asking for help. The church, already reeling from other legal battles, including newly resurfaced child molestation charges within the state of Florida, needed to make this new problem disappear as soon as possible. The orders came swiftly and directly from Rome to quell this issue, and Father Mulligan immediately transferred out of Florida and relocated elsewhere. So, under the cover of night, this was how he came to be transferred to the sleepy parish in Brooklyn, where nobody knew him.

The parishioners here are mostly Black, much different from the primarily Hispanic Caribbean community in South Florida, but still Caribbean people nonetheless. The Irish priest was immediately accepted and embraced by this new community. Father Mulligan has come to care deeply for this community he now serves, and eventually has begun to feel like he could put down roots.

However, with the grounds of the church violently shaking, the sight of this demonic abomination within the church today has obliterated the previous sense of security the Priest felt within this new parish community. Father Mulligan, quickly assessing that this presence is clearly a definite physical and spiritual threat, continues his prayers to dispatch the demon but also begins to look around to see what other protection he could use against this apparent physical threat. He notices a glass canteen filled with holy water falling from one of the shelves behind the altar.

He pulls himself over to it and picks it up. Meanwhile, Michael was roaring and snarling at the priest and continuing to advance forward down the aisle of the church toward the altar, where the priest was lying on the floor after being knocked over by the earthquake.

Aftershocks continue to rumble, shaking the ground and making it difficult for the priest to get back up. When the priest notices that Michael, who is still advancing, has made it up to the third three rows of pews before the stairs leading up to the altar, and close enough, the priest hurls the glass canteen directly at Michael like a grenade. The glass canteen hits Michael square in the face and chest, breaks, and explodes, covering him with holy water. Michael screams in pain as the holy water burns his skin.

"It burns! It burns!" Michael screams in a hoarse, demonic voice.

Fires continue spontaneously igniting around the church, signaling the unholy presence within the church. A NYPD squad car on patrol passing by sees the flames coming out of the front door. The officers are close friends with Father Mulligan, can't believe what they see, and are concerned for the priest's safety. The two officers stop the squad car and run inside to investigate.

The first officer inside the church can't believe what he sees and, strictly on instinct, yells, "Hey! Get away from him!" Michael's head turns 360 degrees around, but without his neck or body moving. Bones within his neck are heard snapping and popping as his head completely turns, and now his face is above his back, and he looks directly and angrily at the cop.

The second officer rushes in and yells, "What the fuck is that?"

"I don't know, light it up!" screams the officer.

Michael is still in a repetitive loop, constantly morphing from demon to human form and back again. The police officers immediately open fire, striking him directly several times, but this does not kill him… Still, in quasi-demon form, Michael turns his head back around, looks up, and leaps forty feet straight up in the air to the ceiling, crashes through a stained-glass window near the highest point of the ceiling, and disappears into the darkness of the night.

They say time heals all wounds. After five days since the supernatural events at the church, Michael's wounds are completely healed. He is the guest of honor at a party held at Bold Advertising to celebrate his acquisition of the Nagasaki account. The mood is festive as champagne flows and an expensive spread of catered food. Roger Freeman and Michael Hill are standing at the head of the conference room table.

"May I have your attention, please? So, the lawyers have worked out all the details, the contract has been officially signed, and I just want to say that in all my years in advertising, I have never seen a natural-born Ad man like this man right here – Mr. Michael Hill!," says Roger.

The employees burst into immediate applause and cheering.

"Thanks to Michael's gifts and talents, we have just closed the largest advertising deal this firm or any other firm in America has ever received with Nagasaki Tires budget valued at 25 million dollars annually!" Roger proclaims.

Again, the employees start applauding and toasting with champagne!

Roger Freeman cuts short this second round of cheering and continues.

"Thanks to Michael, this company's value has gone through the roof, we are in the black, and everyone will be getting a huge bonus this year! Moreover, we will be able to complete the construction on the 33rd Floor, where Michael will have a new office on our new executive floor once it is completed!" yells Roger.

More cheering and applauding!

"And for Michael, for whom none of this would be possible without him… None of it… I am announcing his promotion, effective immediately, to V.P. of Account Services, with a significant increase in pay and, of course, a very attractive bonus. As an extraordinary gift from the Bold family, we are presenting Michael with this Rolex watch, and the inscription on the back reads, "To Michael Hill, The Unicorn & Upwardly Mobile of Bold!" says Roger.

The employees all clap! Messrs Charleswell and Blake from security and the mailroom are also at the party and proud of Michael. Charleswell shakes Michael's hand and comments on the Rolex.

Dirk is wholly diminished and stands alone in the corner of the conference room. From the corner of his eye, Michael notices Tiffany Freeman staring intently at him and smiling…

Michael also sees Buns standing outside the conference room with his mail cart as he rounds around the floor. The expression on his face is not one of joy but one of profound disappointment... Michael continues his speech.

"Thank you! Thank you! I have to start by first thanking Mr. Freeman for the new promotion, and for everything. This is a team effort, so I want to also thank and recognize Jessica and her creative team, as well as all of my colleagues on the account side. We've got a lot of work to do to keep Bold Advertising growing, but with the awesome team that we have, the sky is the limit! May the future for Bold Advertising continue to be bright, lucrative, and never-ending!," Michael yells.

Outside the conference room, Buns looks away sadly and pads his head down, pushing his cart down the aisle.

Michael and Susan have been flirting heavily throughout the party, and an attraction is there. After the party, they sneak away to the 33rd floor, currently under construction. They have both been drinking heavily and are highly intoxicated. The floor is freezing cold as there are several open windows, which still need to be installed.

The floor has construction lights, which have been left on, and white paint drop sheets hanging from the ceiling; this creates an intimate and romantic feel. The two use the light from a construction light projected on a white drop cloth in front of them to generate silhouette shapes using their hands, such as birds flying, a dog, a bunny rabbit, etc. After laughing and enjoying each other's company, Michael and Susan begin passionately kissing and making out. Susan interrupts the kissing.

"Well, congratulations, Mr. VP! Oh my God, you were so dynamic when you closed the Nagasaki account! You were so powerful! So strong!" she states.

"Sounds like I really impressed you?" Michael says.

"Yeah… You definitely did! Ummm… I have a confession to make…"

"Really, what's that?" Michael inquires.

"You had me at hello… I liked you from the minute I first saw you delivering the mail, Mr. Mailman…," Susan confesses, giggling like a schoolgirl.

"Oh, is that right… and you never said anything to me… So, you noticed me, huh? Cause I definitely noticed you…," Michael states.

"Well, I always thought you were handsome, and kind, and so cute, pushing your little mail cart," she laughs playfully.

"Oh…so you were checking for me, huh?" Michael says.

Michael playfully grabs her, they both laugh, and Michael assertively kisses her passionately.

"I need to tell you that I have a lot of things going on right now… So, I'm not really sure if it's a good idea for you to mess with me?" Michael asks.

"I'm a big girl. I'll take my chances," Susan responds.

"Well, if we're making true confessions, I used to love coming to your floor, just so I could see you… I never said anything, but I noticed you right away, and always felt that you were so beautiful…" He kisses her again passionately, losing himself in the beauty of this woman. This time, Michael interrupts the kissing.

"Hey, umm… look… This may sound completely crazy, but why don't you run away with me? We can just run away from all of this together…," he asks.

"Run away? Run away from what? What are you talking about? Run away to go where?" Susan inquires.

"Well, anywhere… I'm serious. Let's just pack up our things and leave, leave the company, leave New York, and just run away together," Michael states.

"So, you're joking, right? Well, for starters, I can't just pack up and leave like that, even if I wanted to. I have my family, my job – and neither can you…," Susan articulates.

She cups his face with both hands and looks deeply into his eyes.

"Look, you're under a lot of pressure, which is completely understandable. But you are just coming into your own, and beginning to climb the corporate ladder, and you're going to go very far – trust me," she tells him.

"But where is all of this negativity coming from? Is this coming from your mailroom friend? What's his name again… "Buns?" she asks.

"This has nothing to do with "Buns!"

"Well, for the record, I don't understand what you see in him anyway. Doesn't he stutter? That guy is such a loser," she says offhandedly.

"Hey! He's not a loser, okay! He's like a brother to me! He stutters occasionally, when he's nervous or agitated, but he's not a loser!" Michael screams, startling Susan in the process. He lowers his voice to almost a whisper once he realizes he has overacted and scares her.

"Look, I wouldn't even be here, at this job if it wasn't for him. It's just… I'm starting to realize that with all this success sometimes things may look a certain way, but then they're really not that way… You know what I mean?" he asks.

"I actually have no idea what you are talking about," she responds.

"I guess I'm just finally realizing that money really can't buy true happiness… and that sometimes what you may think looks good at first really isn't – all that glitters is not gold…," he says, deep in thought.

"What the hell does that mean?"

"It's… It's just something someone told me once…" Michael offers.

"Look, you're red-hot right now. You are the youngest V.P. in the history of this company, and you're the first and only Black executive the company has ever had. Do you realize that? I mean, your rise in this company is completely unheard of... First of all, you're Black, young – this company has never had anyone like you in its upper circles. You have the talent and potential to go to the top. You're making more money than you've probably ever made and have the power and status it takes people a lifetime to achieve. You have the talent to propel this entire company forward at your fingertips, and everybody knows it. Why on earth would you give all of that up? "No, you're staying right where you are, and I'm going to be right here with you at your side," Susan concludes.

"I guess you're right... So, maybe I will stay. But what was that part again about you being right by my side?" Michael playfully asks.

Michael and Susan kiss again and ultimately make passionate love on the floor under the dark sky, under the moon.

As the sun rises on a new day, the morning hides the secrets of the night's activities at Bold. However, the Bold Advertising building and offices are no stranger to romantic interludes, nor is it a stranger to men on a mission. Roger Freeman is walking down the corridor to Michael's cubicle. He knocks on the side panel…

"Good morning, Michael! How is my million-dollar man doing? I must say you're looking quite drippy today. Are you keeping it 100?" says Roger with an impish grin, like a young child who has learned a new word and is eager to use it in any context.

"I am doing well, sir! Thank you for asking, and how are you doing?"

"Couldn't be better, my boy! Michael, congratulations again on this well-deserved promotion. You're the new office unicorn, kid! Let me officially say, that you're beginning your Corporate Climb...," says Roger.

"What is that phrase? When I got the associate's position, Dirk said those exact words. Is that some type of Bold Advertising code phrase or something? He asks.

"Well, it's a phrase I coined way back, when I first started this company, and it has become something of a tradition. Something that older execs tell new execs. It's based on the legend that unicorns are rare and magical. So, that's just my wish for you that you will continue to make magic for Bold Advertising...," Roger explains.

"I see. Well, I will certainly try," says Michael.

"Well, just so you know we are getting your new office ready for you as we speak, so you'll need to get ready to move your things over. You'll also be getting a brand new elegantly crafted mahogany desk just like mine. Consider it, my investment in you. Michael, I can't stop singing your praises. Thanks to you, we have landed one of the biggest accounts on Madison Ave. We have several other major campaigns to pitch or are already in production, all because of you... I want you to know that I have the utmost confidence in you, and that's why I am putting everything in your very capable arms," Roger explains and then continues.

"I want the transition between Dirk's departure and your settling into the role as V.P. to be a smooth one. I've been also thinking that an important man like you should have your own private assistant… Someone to prioritize and manage your schedule. So, I am going to have Maria, the temp we have down at reception on my floor, report to you, and serve as your personal assistant instead…"

"Mr. Freeman, you don't have to do that… I actually don't need a personal assistant…," Michael responds.

"Nonsense, all powerful men have assistants. In fact, she actually used to be my personal assistant off and on… then, ummm… My third and current wife seems to have a problem with her for some… reason… So, we had her transferred to the reception area… but I think that she would be a great help to you and an addition to your team… Think of her as my gift to you… Trust me, you'll thank me later…," Roger says with an impish smile.

"This really isn't necessary…" Michael states, but it is the cost of Roger, who insists.

"It's already done, my boy. We will spare no expense to ensure that you are completely happy, and she starts immediately," Roger offers.

He motions to Maria, and she comes down the aisle with a banker's box of her stuff, waives to Michael, and begins setting up her things at the desk in front of Michael's new office. Of course, both Michael and Buns have noticed and discussed Maria before at length, as she is an attractive forty-something Latina.

"The temp agency is sending a replacement to cover reception on my floor. Like I said, you'll definitely thank me later...," Roger offers.

Later that night. Miss Ella is cleaning up on the 32nd floor. She is alone. She stops by Michael's desk, empties his wastebasket, and cleans his desk. However, she can't help but notice the curious-looking wooden black box on the corner of the desk.... The eyes of the box are shimmering and look like tiny specs of gold glitter. She feels like the box is calling out to her. She can't resist it...

So, she opens the box... As Ella opens the wish box, she is bathed in a blinding light from within the box, accompanied by an audible hum building in intensity, followed by a loud crack, and the box starts angrily vibrating... Startled, she runs away.

Michael arrives at the office at 7:00 a.m. When he gets to the office, he first notices that the wish box on his cubicle desk is wide open on the desk, with the contents in clear view... He frantically closes it and looks around for who did this but sees no one... He does notice some of the building's maintenance men putting up his new nameplate on his new office across the room. There are some boxes on the floor where he has packed his few belongings, primarily manuals and documents. He thinks about what the voodoo man said, "The spirit is giving you much, and in return, you have to give it something back...

If you miss even one day of not giving a sacrifice to the demon, or if you open the box without putting something in… bad things will happen…" Scratch told him.

Michael is interrupted by his thoughts and brought back to reality by one of the movers.

"Excuse me, Mr. Hill, I just wanted to let you know that we've finished setting up your new office. So, we'd like to start moving your things over," the mover says.

"Huh… Yeah… Sure… I don't really have that much, but you can start moving these boxes over at least," Michael responds.

"No problem, Mr. Hill. We'll put your nameplate on your office and everything."

Michael gets up from the desk to give the movers room. As he gets up, he notices Dirk staring at him from his office. Michael stands his ground and looks at him directly.

Dirk begins clapping slowly and deliberately… He is now looking and acting like his old self again. This is a result of the wish box being opened by Ella and no offerings being placed within the box for 24 hours, nullifying the original binding curse placed on him.

"Well, well… if it isn't our new rockstar… Congratulations little Mikey… well done… Oh, by the way, I know that it was you who sent those photocopies of me and Tiffany to Roger… I have to say that I really underestimated you, mail boy… You really played your hand well… But just remember that the game isn't over yet…and this is still my yard!" Dirk says in a venomous tone.

"Is that supposed to be some kind of threat? First off, I don't know what photocopies you're talking about. Second, you've got some balls on you, to try to talk to me like that, given your situation," Michael responds.

"You're quite the climber, aren't you boy? I mean coming all the way up from the mailroom to the very pinnacle of the company… But remember that I brought you here. You want to be me so badly, don't you? I wasn't feeling quite like myself the past few days, wasn't thinking straight… But I want you to know that I'm back now, and I definitely see you…," Dirk says.

Michael glances from the side of his eyes at the open wooden box on his desk, which he does not want Dirk to see…

"You may think you're clever and that you've won because you've taken my job…taken my livelihood…and humiliated me. But trust me, it's far over… This is just the beginning… I got my eyes on you." he says cryptically.

Dirk walks backward into his office, never looking at Michael, and closes the door.

14 THE INVESTIGATION

Michael is sitting at his desk, and his eyes turn black, confirming his demonic possession. His face looks evil, with sharp, jagged fangs and teeth protruding from his mouth. His face has healed from the burns due to the holy water. There is a knock on his door. The metamorphosis begins to reverse itself, but he develops a nosebleed, which he tries desperately to stop. Thick black blood begins to ooze from his right nostril. The person on the other side of the door is impatient. The doorknob continuously turns, but the door is locked. Michael is still in a quasi-pre-demonic state and needs more time to turn back. His claws have changed since, and his jagged fangs are just beginning to give way to his human teeth. He can finally stop the nosebleed, wipe away the blood using his sleeve, and fumble around to compose himself.

"Just a minute..." Michael says.

He gets up to open the door. Standing at the door is Tiffany Freeman. Tiffany is radiant and stunning with her Marilyn Monroe look and vibe. Michael can definitely see why Betancourt is attracted to her.

"Hi, Michael it's me Tiffany, can I come in?"

"Yeah, of course. I'm sorry, I was just finishing a report," he says, unlocking the door and opening it, and she enters the office, looking around to figure out what he was really doing.

"I hope I'm not bothering you… I just wanted to stop by to say hi and to congratulate you again on landing the Nagasaki account," Tiffany says.

"Thank you, Tiffany, it means a lot to me coming from you," Michael says.

"I haven't seen my father this happy, in a very long time. You have dramatically changed everything around here. I mean, it's great. The electricity is in the air in terms of the opportunities ahead of us. So, I would really like the opportunity to work closely with you on the work you're doing. I mean if you'll let me," she says softly.

Michael pauses.

"I don't have a problem with that," Michael states.

"Great! I'm really looking forward to it. Maybe we can discuss it some more over dinner?" she coyly adds.

"I really don't have much time for dinner lately," Michael counters.

"Totally understand. I mean that's how you've become so great right, because you're always working and perfecting your craft right? I mean, I get it, but I mean you still have to eat right?"

Michael begins to sense where this conversation is going and feels slightly uncomfortable.

"Yeah maybe… umm… look, if you don't mind, I'm on deadline for a report I have due," Michael says, moving towards the door to show her out.

"Yeah, okay, I don't want to hold you up. So, I'll see you later?" she asks.

"Yeah. Thanks for stopping by," Michael states.

Tiffany exits the office very quickly and accidentally runs right into Jimmy, who is walking past the office, causing the stack of papers he was carrying to fall and scatter…

"Oh my God… I am so sorry…," Tiffany offers.

"Oh… that's okay, Tiffany… It was my fault… I didn't notice where I was…," Jimmy awkwardly gushes.

However, Tiffany does not even bother to help pick up the papers and has already walked away and tuned out before Jimmy can even finish speaking…

Nighttime arrives once again, bathing NYC in darkness. New York may not be much to look at in the daytime. However, at night, the lights across the city and skyline genuinely make the town look beautiful. Looking at the city from up high or overhead, the lights illuminate and look like tiny specs of shimmering glitter.

Michael is working at his computer and getting into a good workflow rhythm. He is pounding vigorously at his keyboard and getting much work done. He has begun to let a beard come in, making him look older and more distinguished. He is dressed in an expensive black suit, dark tie, glasses, and Rolex. His office and attire have all the material trappings of success. Yet he has an empty, hollow, and hardened look. He has faint dark circles now appearing under his eyes.

Maria, Michael's new secretary, silently comes into the office, closes the door, lowers the shades, comes right up to the desk, smiles, and then gets down on her hands and knees and goes under the desk… the sound of a zipper being pulled down is heard. However, Michael never misses a beat and continues working on his desktop.

Dirk has been watching all of this from the cubicle pool nearby, just outside of his office, and can't pull himself away from watching…most of the employees on the floor have already left by this time.

However, Jimmy comes down the aisle, sees Dirk standing there, and comes up to him.

"Hey Dirk, I know it's late, but have you seen Maria, I have some documents I owe her. Have you seen her, is she around?"

Dirk answers sarcastically and dryly.

"She's around, but I believe she's taking dictation right now...," he answers mockingly.

Dirk turns around, stone-faced and walks away. Jimmy has a puzzled and confused look on his face...

Later that night, Michael is still at his desk working. Maria has long since left. However, his stomach starts to growl very loudly, as if he's famished, but the sounds he hears are not normal... He quickly gets up from his desk and runs to the bathroom. The lights begin flickering wildly. He runs in and pushes open a stall door. He immediately drops to the floor, his stomach heaves, and he throws up. He looks down at the excessive amount of sticky, black, ink-like vomit he threw up in the toilet, containing ears, eyes, and two fingers. Then, when he raises his head, his eyes become black, and his body begins to convulse and change... agonizing pain causes his body to violently shake. He grabs at his suit and clothes, tearing them off. Standing naked and panting heavily and erratically. He falls to his hands and knees and begins to change. The metamorphosis from man to a bestial demon is not an easy one. His face begins to morph, taking on an evil devilish appearance as his nose and mouth begin to protrude and extend out. His eyes go from being completely black in the early stage of the possession and transformation to now turning completely red in his evolving demonic monster state. As muscle and bone snap and reform, his body suffers lacerating pain.

Michael's flesh changes color and texture to a jet-black color. The skin around his chest and torso becomes tight against his bones, giving him an utterly skeletal-like appearance. His mouth bleeds profusely as jagged fangs emerge. His whole face distorts as his jaw freakishly extends, and rows of ragged teeth appear book-ended by long, sharp fangs. His skull bubbles and from the crown of his head emerges a large singular elongated demonic ram horn. His fingers stretch and mutate into sharp claws. The transformation process is graphic and painful as he transforms from human into complete demon form. He is a true monster in every definition of the word.

Ms. Ella has just finished cleaning and is at the elevator bank waiting for it to come. The door opens, and she steps inside with her cleaning items. Just then, the bathroom door opens, and the demon runs at lightning speed and reaches the elevator door just as it closes. The demon pries the outer elevator door open and sees that the elevator has already descended downwards. The demon jumps into the elevator shaft and lands on top of the elevator just as the doors open to let Ella out on the floor below. The elevator rocks violently when the demon lands on the top of the elevator. Ella looks up at the elevator ceiling and is startled. She quickly moves out of the elevator, and the door closes. Suddenly, she is overcome by the smell of a strong, rancid, and foul odor, and she takes a handkerchief from her apron and places it over her nose. She stands looking at the closed elevator door. She is afraid. But after waiting awhile and seeing nothing happen, she pushes her cart forward and moves toward the far corner of the floor to begin cleaning. The lights are all on automatic sensors. So, the whole floor is dark, except for the sections where she is walking. When she gets to the far corner. She hears the elevator door open and close… She looks into the vast darkness behind her but sees no one.

"Hello? Who's there?" Ella asks. However, there has yet to be a response. So, Ella then turns the vacuum on and begins cleaning. However, as she is doing so, in the windows of the offices, she can see that the overhead lights are coming on, section by section coming towards her… However, although the lights are coming on, they are also flickering and dimming when they are on, which she has never seen happen before.

"Hello? Who's there? I'm going to call security…," she says firmly.

She hears a low, menacing, guttural growl.

"Oh God…," she says aloud.

She starts running at top speed, but the demon is in fast pursuit. The demon's bright red eyes locked in on her every step.

She runs as fast as she can around the circular layout of the floor to head back towards the elevator. The lights go completely out. She reaches the elevator bank when the demon leaps and pounces on her just as the elevator door opens. She screams in pain as the monster rips her heart, eats it while it is still beating, and repeatedly bites chunks of flesh from her body, swallowing whole pieces of her. He consumes most of her body and leaves a complete mess of what's left. The demon then bites off her finger from her hand, removes Ella's ring, rushes off to the stairs, exits the building from a back exit, and runs into the night.

Early the following day, multiple police cruisers parked in front of the Bold Advertising Building. Police tape has the entire sidewalk blocked off in front of the building. Pedestrians on the street are talking and pointing at the facility, speculating what may be happening inside. The television news units are starting to arrive at the same time and begin setting up to transmit the day's breaking news – there has been a violent murder at Bold Advertising.

The elevator doors open on the floor, and out steps Roger Freeman along with his daughter Tiffany.

"What happened here?" Roger demands.

"I gave strict orders to security that no one was supposed to be let up here. And who are you?" Detective Soto asks.

"I'm Roger Freeman, CEO, and owner of the company. What is going on here?" Roger asks again.

"Well sir, it appears that one of your employees, one of your cleaning ladies, was killed last night!" Soto says.

"Oh, dear God… Killed? Here? Roger responds.

"Yeah. We need you to take a look to help us identify her. I have to first warn you that it is not a pretty sight…" With that, he lifts the sheet placed over the deceased. He lifts the sheet, Roger gasps, and Tiffany winces at the gruesome sight of the body, which has been wholly mutilated and is mainly just half a torso, with a severed arm and a missing ring finger…

"Oh God, its Ella! Her name is Ella Mae Leonard," she was one of our cleaning ladies." Roger states and holds his head down, looking away as he is rattled by the situation.

Tiffany buries her face into her dad's coat and cries…

"Mr. Freeman there are bite marks all over the body…and chunks of her are completely missing, like something literally ate her… Her arm was pulled off, and it looks like her ring finger was bitten off… I mean if I didn't know better, it looks like she was literally attacked and eaten by some type of wild animal… Do you have or know of anyone who is keeping a wild animal of any kind within the building?" Soto asks.

"Absolutely not! That's absurd! Animals are not allowed, and certainly nothing that could do something like this," Roger replies.

"Okay, okay. So, this attack is identical to that wild animal attack in the subway that recently happened… But, considering the fact that we are on the fifteenth floor of a skyscraper in Manhattan, and you said no one has any wild animals here. The question is how a wild animal would get up here on its own?" Soto says.

Roger shrugs, not knowing how to respond to the statement.

"Okay. So, there's another possibility that a two-legged animal or someone − as opposed to something… did this to her…and as incredible as it may seem our suspect could very well be one of your employees… and as a result your company is a part of this person's hunting grounds… So, it's my job to find that someone… How many floors does your company have in this building?" Soto inquires.

"We occupy floors 15 − 32 including the basement level, and the 33rd floor is under construction," Roger states.

"Awesome! So, we're going to have forensics analyze these bite wounds to determine what or who did this to her. In the meantime I'm going to need a complete list of all the employees who currently work on those floors, including the bio-clock read-out of all the employees who were in the office that day, I also need to get a readout of all of your bio badges for all of your doors, and we are trying to obtain the footage from your camera systems right now…," Soto says.

Roger gestures and points to a lady walking towards them, "Ms. Hawkins our HR Director, will provide you with the employee list, and everything you need," Roger proclaims.

"Excellent! Ms. Hawkins, can I just follow you to your office?" Soto asks.

Ms. Hawkins and Detective Soto walk away, headed towards her office. Mr. Freeman is standing in a fog, watching what's left of the body, with dozens of police around him doing various things. He is completely stunned and can't believe what has happened. Meanwhile, Tiffany has taken an elevator up to the 32nd floor.

It's still early in the morning. However, word of Ella's death has spread like wildfire. She was well-known and well-liked by everyone within the company. As a result, the day has been fiercely interrupted. Those employees who were already in the building have been asked to remain so that the police can interview them, but the majority of the employees who either are outside on the sidewalk, unable to enter the building, or even working remotely from home have all been dismissed for the day, due to what has happened. The email going out to the entire staff was not specific, but only stated that a police investigation was underway and asked only for essential employees to come into the office. Police are still walking around, and the offices of Bold are still very much a crime scene.

The elevator door opens, and Tiffany bolts straight toward Michael's office.

The blinds to his office are down, so people on the outside can't see in. She bolts through the door, and he looks up… He is staring blankly at the wish box on his desk.

"Oh, Michael, thank God you're here! Did you hear… did you hear what happened to Ella?" Tiffany asks, tears streaming down her face.

Michael is obviously aware of what happened but plays dumb…

"No, I didn't, I got in very early to finish some work. What's going on? I saw the police and the commotion looking out from my window, but wasn't sure what was going on?" Michael says.

"Ella is dead! Ms. Ella is dead! Somebody killed her, and just ripped her apart. It's so horrible...," Tiffany shouts.

She throws herself into Michael's arms.

"Okay, okay... calm down...it's going to be alright.... Shhhh.... Shhhh...," Michael comforts her.

"So, do the police know what happened? What did they say?" asks Michael; within his mind, the fear of being caught by the police and exposed for what he has become runs over and over his mind.

"They don't know. They said it looked like some kind of wild animal ripped her apart and ate her... Which makes no sense! She was the sweetest person, wouldn't hurt a fly... Why? I don't understand why...," she states.

Tiffany starts sobbing loudly. Michael embraces her tightly and tries to comfort her. After a while, she looks up into his face and starts to kiss him passionately, and he reciprocates a bit before eventually pulling away...

"Ummm... Look you should go...," Michael says.

"Why? I see the way you look at me… Don't you want me?" she asks him, her voice quickly pivoting from sadness to one oozing with seduction.

"Are you afraid of my father? Is that it? Don't be; I'm a grown woman who makes her own decisions. Besides, he doesn't care… He doesn't care about anything except for money and this damn company… We could be together if you want. Wouldn't you like that? I know I would…," she says, pushing her torso towards his. He gently pushes her away.

"It's not that, but we're just friends, that's all…," Michael says.

Tiffany pauses, feeling a bit annoyed.

"It's because of her, isn't it… it's because of Susan, right?" she demands angrily.

Michael is shocked at her tone and that she is aware of his interest in Susan.

"What are you talking about?" he says.

She interrupts, "Don't lie, you think I don't know… Everyone knows. So, you want her, right, but you don't want me, is that it?

She pauses, looks him directly in the eyes, and says, "So, what if I told you that you could have both of us… Would that make you happy?" she coos seductively.

"I think you should go now," Michael says firmly.

Sensing his resolve, she reverts back to her normal voice and posture.

"I can make you happy, and I am going to make you want me, if it's the last thing I do," she says.

"Goodbye, Tiffany," Michael demands.

She sees the stern look on his face and closes the door. He turns out the lights, locks the door, and sits down in his chair, wholly spent over everything that has happened. He looks at the box on his desk, opens it, and sees Ms. Ella's ring in the wish box, with the ring still on the finger. He has a flashback of savagely biting and eating Ms. Ella in demon form. But then he also has a flashback and recalls Ms. Ella's words...

"All that glitters is not gold..."

He reflects on those words as he now has everything he could ever want: money, power, influence, his choice of women... And while it all seems attractive and glittery at first glance, the tie to all of this is predicated on murder, cannibalism, and evil. He remembers killing and savaging Ms. Ella – his friend. He remembers eating her body and flesh. He is completely repulsed by what he did...but more importantly, he realizes that what Ms. Ella told him is the same thing he now realizes was what was being whispered over and over in his dream involving his dad – "All that glitters is not gold..."

"Oh God… what have I done… Ms. Ella… "I'm so sorry, Ms. Ella; you didn't deserve this… I'm sorry… I'm so sorry…" he begins to sob profusely, struggling under the enormous weight of his guilt for what he did. As a result of the curse of the wish box, he is a deeply conflicted man, on the one hand handsomely rewarded by his contract with the wish box, and at the same time saddened and repulsed by what he has done. More importantly, he recognizes that Ella is his third victim, placing him closer to acknowledging the evil and eternal damnation prophecy of the wish box – being forever permanently transformed into a demon.

He quickly grabs his things and uses the back stairs to the ground level. When he gets to the rear door exit, there's a cop there, but he is urinating against the wall in the far corner of the stair exit, so he does not see Michael quietly slip out the back door, leaving the building just as the police are assertively arriving on his floor to begin questioning of the employees, literally missing the fleeing Michael by just minutes.

The police have interfaced with Mr. Charleswell, the head of Bold Security, and are actively reviewing security camera footage from the floor on which the incident occurred last night. Detective Soto is heading up the investigation, assisted by Officer Rizzo, the first officer on the scene when the initial call came to 911 when another cleaning crew found the body.

Soto is addressing Officer Rizzo and asks, "First thing first. You completely locked down the building like I asked, right?" Soto asks.

"Yes, all ingress and egress points are covered! No one is getting in or out of this building unless we check them... We have to catch this sick son of a bitch if he's still here...," Rizzo states.

"Oh, you have my word, if the suspect is here, we'll get him one way or the other, this place is crawling with cops. The M.O. of that wild animal killing in the subway, and the murder here, are identical. So, we definitely have some type of serial pattern on our hands, and my gut is telling me that this company is somehow the link that ties them all together. So, we need to review the security footage with a fine-tooth comb...," Soto says.

Charleswell has teed up the requested footage on the big monitor screen within the security room of the company.

"So, here's all the security footage we have from last night," Charleswell exclaims.

"Okay, so what am I looking at here... I want to see footage from the 15th Floor, starting at 5:00 pm onwards.", Soto says.

They see various employees leaving, and the floor becomes emptier and emptier. Finally, it's at 12:00 am, and we see Ms. Ella come off the elevator pushing her cleaning basket and equipment...

"Whoa...whoa... slow it down right here... there's our girl... but what's she doing?" Soto asks.

"She just got off the elevator, but she looks scared… Now, from her facial expression, it looks like she just smelled something horrible or something…," Rizzo states.

"Show us the footage from the elevator," says Soto, directly to Charleswell.

"Here it is, it's clear, there's nobody in there other than her," says Charleswell.

"What about on top?" Soto asks.

"What do you mean on top?" Charleswell says, trying to understand what the Detective is referring to.

Do you have footage that provides a view from the top of the elevator? Like in the elevator shaft?" Soto asks.

"Unfortunately, no," Charleswell confirms.

"Well, from the looks of things, she either saw or heard something in that elevator, we need to know what that was," Soto states.

They continue looking at the security video playback.

Rizzo references what he sees: "So, now she's moving deeper into the floor, we see the automatic lights go on in every section she steps into…"

"Yeah, the motion detection sensors for the lights," Charleswell responds.

"Okay, so we see the light sensors turning on the lights in the areas where she is stepping into, but what's happening back there... do you see that? The motion sensor lights are being activated over here behind her, on the other end of the floor, but they seem to be flickering around and blinking, why are they doing that?" Soto asks.

"You're right," Rizzo chimes in.

"There's someone or something on the floor with her now, and whatever it is got off of the same elevator she was on," Soto speculates.

They then see Ms. Ella running back over to the elevator banks, but when she gets there, the tape glitches...and they don't know what attacked her as it lunged and pulled her out of view of the camera.

"Rewind that – play that back!" Soto yells.

The video is rewound, but each time they come to the specific and critical time when the murder occurred, the tape glitches over and goes black.

"I don't understand, there seems to be some type of glitch right at the moment of impact, so we can't see anything," says Charleswell.

"Interesting.... This is exactly what was reported over at the subway killings... We kept that out of the news reports, but the witnesses at the subway killings also reported flickering lights and power outages, and the videotapes from the platform were also mysteriously blurred at the time of the killings... This just keeps getting better and better...

Rizzo, get this tape over to the FBI's crime lab for further analysis. See, if they can correct the glitch. Meanwhile, I want the list from the lobby, as well as everyone who is on all the floors within the building, checked and crosschecked. We are going to interview every single person in this building! One of them has to have seen or heard something. Charleswell, I need you to keep going through the footage of the other floor, see if you can find anything else of interest, or that would give us any further clues," Soto says.

Being utterly distraught over what he has done, Michael has been riding the transit system back and forth, staring blindly ahead, not really taking in anything around him. He is a man drowning in his own damnation. A transit cop enters the train car he is in, and Michael's heart begins pounding rapidly as if it will literally bust out of his chest. Based on the noticeable increased police presence, which he knows is not accidental, he feels the pressure of the police dragnet closing in on him as another cop enters from the opposite side of the train car. He puts his head down and looks away from the officers. At the next stop, the cops both leave the train and get on the platform. Michael breathes a sigh of exhausted relief. After a while, eventually, he passes out due to sheer exhaustion and stress.

He is awakened by an MTA transit conductor yelling at him to wake up and that he is in the train-yard at the end of the stop. Luckily, he is in Brooklyn, so he stumbles off the train and makes his way out of the train yard to the street level, where he catches a gypsy cab to take him home.

The night air brings a sudden flurry of snowflakes, leading to a light dusting of snow blanketing the ground.

The ride home in the cab is uneventful, and when he arrives, Michael opens the door to his apartment and goes inside. He goes to the refrigerator, opens the door wide, and grabs a beer. He walks over into the corner and presses play on his answering machine. It's his mother:

"Michael, thank you so much for the money you sent me! I really appreciate it, but son you sent me so much! Well, I was able to pay the mortgage for the month and all of the utilities, and still had plenty left over to go food shopping… I don't know what to say, except thank you, Son. I love you so much. Call me please when you get a chance, I appreciate the money, but I want to see you as well. Call me please."

15 DOUBLE HOMICIDE

After listening to the message from his mother, the machine clicks off. Michael goes back to the refrigerator and opens the door wide once again. He is feeling more than hungry; he is feeling completely ravenous. The fridge is mostly empty. However, there is some open raw meat on the second shelf that he looks at… Then, he closes the door and walks away. He stops in his tracks, rushes back to the refrigerator, opens it, tears the meat's wrapping, smears the blood all over his face, and then drinks it before savagely gorging himself on the packaged meat. However, it is not satisfying as it is not fresh, and it is not human… His face is completely covered in blood, his eyes turn black, and he then aggressively morphs and changes… His transformation is graphic and gory as he turns from human to demon. He undergoes excruciating pain. As he mutates into the demon monster, his eyes then turn blood-red. Once the change is complete, the hideous demon opens the living room window, which is on the back side of the house, and defies gravity as it crawls down the external wall of the building into an alley at the back of the building. There in the shadows, it moves silently and then waits... An Uber pulls up and discharges two women in front of the building down the street from Michael's building, which is not well-lit in the show. The women are scantily clad, like they just came from a nightclub. They are both giggling and have had far too much to drink.

"Wow… Thank God for Uber!" says Mallory.

"I know that's right…," says Chivon. "Bitch, please, we would have been home hours ago if your so-called boyfriend hadn't started a fight with you and acted like a jerk at the club!" She is wearing a pink, fluorescent wristband from the club.

"Will you please get over yourself? It's over… Okay… So, why don't you just go to your apartment, and I'll go to mine, and we don't have to deal with each other, okay," says Mallory, wearing a gold necklace with a green, fluorescent ID wristband.

"That's fine by me!" says Chivon, suddenly holding her nose. "What is that smell?"

The girls, one White and one of East-Indian descent, both smell an extremely rotten and unpleasant odor. They hear a guttural growl and movement in the side alley…

"So, what the fuck was that?" says Mallory.

"I don't know…" Chivon faces the alley and shouts, "Hey, asshole, we hear you over there! So, stop fucking around, or we'll call the cops! I'm not fuckin kiddin!" states Chivon boldly.

Chivon shines the light from her iPhone into the darkness and sees nothing. However, the power on her phone and the surrounding streetlights start blinking wildly, and eventually, all shut-off, startling the women and leaving them in complete darkness. The women now clearly hear angry snarling and roaring coming towards them. They both look at each other.

Mallory yells, "Shit! Run!"

They both take off and begin running fast towards the front door, but it is a walk-up and some distance away. They turn around and see a dark, monstrous figure on all fours behind them. They scream and begin running at top speed, but Chivon trips and falls down mid-way. Mallory keeps running, makes it to the door, gets in, and runs up the stairs. Chivon runs up to the front door, but as soon as she gets to it, she is grabbed violently from the back, stabbed by the elongated claw, and then bitten and clawed repeatedly right in front of the door.

Mallory continues running up the stairs, screaming. She reaches her door, pushes in her key, and enters her apartment.

Meanwhile, after gorging on large amounts of Chivon outside and dispatching its fourth victim, the demon rejoices internally as it takes its fourth victim and artifact. It then crashes through the downstairs door and bolts up the stairs in pursuit. Mallory is screaming loudly for help and running, and the demon is not far behind.

She is screaming and knocking on doors as she runs, but no one opens the door or comes outside to help her. She finally arrives at her door, fumbling with her keys in the lock, and ultimately pushes the door open, runs in, and locks it. However, almost instantly, she can hear when the demon arrives at her door. It is breathing loudly outside the door and scraping its claws against it.

But after a while, it goes away, and she does not hear the breathing anymore… She takes her cell phone out of her coat pocket and calls 911.

"911. What is your emergency?" the emergency operator says.

"Oh God, something is chasing me!" she screams into the phone.

"Who's chasing you, ma'am! "Ma'am?" the operator demands.

"That thing…that thing… is chasing me, it got Chivon! You should have seen its eyes… its eyes…it was like the devil… Oh God, please hurry!" She pleads.

"Ma'am we're dispatching the police now, where are you?"

"I am showing your address as at 555 Utica Ave. Brooklyn! Help is on the way! Are you safe where you are?" the operator asks.

"I'm in my apartment… Hurry please!"

"Okay, help is on the way. Stay where you are, they will be there soon… stay on the line with me! What's your name?" the operator asks.

"Mallory! Mallory Granger!" She is crying and pleading. "Please hurry!"

However, unseen by Mallory, the demon stealthily crawls up the building wall to where the girl's living room window is located. She is facing the front door and does not see the demon is now on her fire escape balcony. The creature carefully and quietly pries open the window… It is now literally in the apartment… It slyly creeps up behind her and stands up behind her, dwarfing her size. However, the girl notices the reflection in a mirror in front of her, the monstrous demon; she screams and tries to run for the front door. The demon lunges after her and bites her savagely, devouring the victim's flesh savagely.

"Ma'am… ma'am… hello…are you alright? The police are there! They're pulling up outside your building right now, and coming to your apartment? Ma'am can you hear me? Ma'am?"

But there is no response to the questions, only dead silence…

After it quickly eats its fill of the girl, the demon snatches her gold chain as its artifact and prize – thereby advancing the wish box death count to five. The demon then swiftly goes back outside and stealthily climbs the wall to the roof, jumps to an adjacent top, and runs into the night.

The police arrive at the apartment door just minutes later and forcibly kick the door in, only to find the already dead and mutilated girl lying in the living room… Officer Rizzo is one of the officers on the scene. He immediately marks the m.o. of these murders as a very familiar but sad sight… The police establish the crime scene and search around the building and in the alley behind the building in a dumpster; they find the sparse remains of the missing police officer from the subway killing wrapped in a blanket and the cover to a nearby manhole slightly placed to the side. Rizzo pulls out his cell phone…

"Hey, Detective Soto! Yeah, this is Officer Rizzo… Look uh… I think I have something you need to see…. We have a double homicide here in Brooklyn that looks like the same exact MO as the Subway and the Bold Advertising homicides, and umm. We found the body, or what's left of him, of the cop from the subway killing in a dumpster behind the same building as this double homicide… You were right, we definitely have a serial killer on our hands…," Rizzo says.

16 ENOUGH

Michael awakens in his studio, naked, disoriented, and sweaty. He looks at the box and sees the new additions of one pink ID wristband and one gold chain named "Melody." He is fully aware of what he did to get these items… He feels something in his mouth and uses his finger to pull out a partial piece of an index finger with fingernail polish still on it and throws it to the ground. His stomach heaves, and he vomits a copious amount of thick, black, sticky, ink-like vomit. He starts to cry, and the thick, black, ink-like substance also streams from his tears down his face, making him look clown-like.

He begins to panic as he realizes he is on the precipice of becoming forever trapped in demonic form. He wonders what that would be like and what would happen to him afterward. He feels regret at all that he has achieved materially in exchange for the evil he has had to engage in; at the same time, he has become addicted to the rewards of his sin.

He wonders – how can he possibly go on like this? In a fit of rage, he picks up his wish box, throws it in a wastebasket, grabs some lighter fluid along with matches from the kitchen drawer, drenches the wish box with fluid, lights the match, and tosses it on the box. Instantly, the box ignites, but it does not burn… However, his skin suddenly bursts into white-hot flames, and his flesh starts burning. He screams and writhes in pain, kicks the basket over, and uses a blanket to put out the fire on the box, which then extinguishes the flame that has also engulfed him.

Desperate, he enters the bathroom and gets a razor blade from the medicine cabinet. Looking into the mirror, he pauses and then takes the razor and slits both of his wrists deeply…he falls to the floor and rapidly bleeds out black-colored blood. However, as the blood oozes out and pools on the floor, the wounds suddenly heal as if nothing happened… His eyes are wide in complete disbelief; he pulls himself up and staggers back to the mirror over the sink. In the mirror, instead of his reflection, he sees the demon looking back at him with black eyes, breathing hard, snarling, and leering at him. He angrily punches the mirror, shattering it and grabbing one of the shards of glass. He runs out of the bathroom aggressively, grabs his coat, puts the glass in his coat pocket, and bolts out of the front door.

It's incredible how fast you can drive on a mission. Michael has run through several traffic lights and is gunning the car's engine, speeding down the streets of Brooklyn. It is snowing quite heavily, and he is lucky that it is late at night, and he manages to avoid being detected by law enforcement. Michael's car pulls up in front of Scratch's building. He is driving a new all-black Series 7 BMW with Nagasaki tires and rims. The license plate reads "Drip 1." He is dressed in all black. He walks up to the building and tries to enter, but the front external door is locked. So, in a desperate attempt to gain access, he presses all the intercom buzzers; distorted voices answer and one buzzes him in. He runs to the staircase and goes down into the basement. He comes to the door and knocks lightly…

"Speak!" Scratch's booming voice commands.

"It's me, Philbert…," Michael says softly through the door.

"Philbert?" Scratch repeats, trying to think why Philbert would be coming by at this hour.

Scratch opens the door slightly, using his hand to secure the security chain at the top of the door, but Michael takes the shard of mirror glass from his pocket, stabs it into Scratch's hand, and then kicks the door in. Scratch falls to the floor, screaming in pain, and pulls the glass out of his hand. However, Michael seizes the opportunity and jumps on top of him, punching him repeatedly in the face.

"You! You son of a bitch! You been fucking wid' me for a long time, haven't you? Coming into my family's house when my father died! Coming into my dreams in my apartment, you son of a bitch! That was all you, wasn't it? You did all this to me! You brought me into your web, then sold me to the devil – with your damn wish box. You turned me into this – into a monster! This isn't what I asked for! I don't want the damned box or none of the shit it gives you… I want my soul back! I want my life back! You hear me! Remove the curse!" he yells.

The two struggle violently, eventually falling to the floor, but Scratch will not be taken quickly and gets the advantage on top of Michael, punching him several times in the face.

"Get off me! Get the fuck off me!" Michael knees Scratch in the groin, and as the older man doubles over. Michael quickly grabs him by the throat and pins him to the wall, his hand transforming into demon form. However, Scratch's eyes illuminate and turn bright white, and he gestures to the far wall, causing the demon portal to become illuminated. Some demons are already waiting at the front of the portal.

Scratch yells, "Louvri pòt la," ("Open the portal" – Patois translation). "Help me, Brothers! Cross over and kill him!!!," Scratch commands.

Three demons immediately cross over the portal and into the air as wisps of ectoplasm and fire. The evil faces within the ectoplasm are screaming and wailing. They fly up to the top of the ceiling and fly around in a circle. Seeing them, Michael releases his grip, and Scratch falls to the floor. The demons then circle above Michael at incredible speeds, criss-crossing, hissing, screaming, flying around him, biting and visibly scratching his flesh, drawing blood. Michael sees a machete on the floor, picks it up, and swings at the demons, but it goes through them and does not affect them. He then grabs Scratch, lifts him up, and puts the sharp blade of the machete to his jugular.

"Call them off! Call them off now, dammit! Do it, or I swear, I'll cut your fucking throat! Do it now!" Michael demands.

Scratch, seeing little options out of this situation, complies.

"Brothers stop! It's okay… it's okay… Enter the wish boxes, and await your human hosts…," Scratch assures the demons.

The demons halt their assault and follow the instructions, entering three wish boxes on the floor. However, the lead demon in hell, Congo Savanne, has been watching these actions through the portal window and, sensing a potential and unwanted interruption in the demonic pipeline, begins running towards the portal, first on two legs, then switching to running on all fours like an animal. His huge ram's head and gigantic demonic frame barreled quickly toward the portal window. He reaches the window and begins to push his enormous clawed hand through the portal. Michael is watching with horror as he sees the giant demon beginning to push its claw through the portal.

"Close that fucking devil window! Now! Do it!" Michael demands.

Scratch hesitates at first, but then reluctantly complies as the blade begins to cut into his throat. He gestures counterclockwise, closing the portal window.

"Okay…okay…Fèmen pòt la," (Close the portal – Patios translation), Scratch says.

However, Congo Savanne's elongated digits are already through the portal as it begins to close. The portal closes around the gigantic demon's hand, which is on the earthly side of the portal, and severs the demon's fingers as it approaches. A distorted and unholy howl is heard from the demon as the portal closes, and the severed fingers drop to the floor, turning into a rotting pile of maggots and worms. A disembodied, distorted, and demonic voice eerily warns, "You will never escape my grasp…never!"

Michael punches Scratch hard to the jaw, knocking him down. Once on the floor, he relentlessly kicks him several times in the face and stomach, pulls him back up, and throws him back against the wall.

"You full of tricks, ain't you? Fuckin voodoo witch, devil, or whatever the fuck you are… You're going to make all of this shit you've done to me, stop! You hear me?" yells Michael.

"I can't stop it – you made a wish and a deal… spitting blood and several teeth. You made a contract with the dark one – and you received everything you wanted, spoken and unspoken. You are bound to him forever! You heard him – he will never let you go!" Scratch yells.

"No! I didn't wish for any of this! What I wished for was to have my boss stop fucking with me! That's it! Instead, you gave me riches and material success as a bonus, but then neglected to fully mention the fucked upside effects! I have already killed and eaten five people! I can't control this never-ending, ravenous hunger for flesh and blood I have all the time! I have to kill, eat the flesh of my victims, and put an item that belonged to them in that damn box just so that I can have a day or two of normalcy. Only to repeat the same thing over and over again… I want success – but not like this! I'm not going to live the rest of my life like this! You hear me! Take this curse off me now!" Michael again demands.

"I told you I can't…the dark one owns your soul now, there is nothing you can do!" Scratch says defiantly.

"That's bullshit! There has to be a way!" Michael replies.

Viciously grabbing him and choking him, his hands turning into demonic claws, and his face morphing into the demon… Fear is now in Scratch's eyes as he realizes he is in a no-win position. However, he suddenly starts incoherently laughing while also coughing.

"Okay, okay, I'll tell you… You're already dead anyway… Only…" He starts to say something but then stops…

"Only what? Only what, you son of a bitch? I'll kill you! What is it? Say it dammit!"

He starts punching Scratch several times in the face…bloody and dazed, he relents, sensing that his life is clearly in jeopardy by a man who has been pushed beyond his limits.

"Wait…wait… I'll… I'll…tell you… The only way… to stop it… is…is to gift the curse to someone else…," utters Scratch.

"Give it to someone else?" Michael asks.

"No, *gift* it to someone else… You would need to present it to them as a gift, which they willingly accept. Then once they puncture their hand on the lid, the box then becomes theirs, and the curse is transferred from you to the other person. But the dark lord does not like loose ends… The loss of even one soul is a loose end…and he will never stop until he retrieves that soul back. So, the gifting may not work… It is impossible to escape his grasp. He will never let you go…," Scratch concludes.

"I'll take my chances," Michael snaps.

"You will have to do it before you kill six times… You said you have already killed five times… So, one more kill, and you will become forever trapped in demon form…you will never change back to human. The demon inside you knows this, and so it will purposefully increase your hunger for flesh to force you to kill one more time, so that it can collect your soul. Be warned, if you gift the box to someone else, or if the original cursed person dies, it angers the demon, because it interrupts the curse. If that happens the demon will not abide by the normal rules of the wish box, it will then become desperate, lash out, become uncontrollable, and quickly possess anyone it can, at any cost," Scratch concedes.

Michael swings and punches Scratch hard to the jaw, knocking him completely out.

It is 4:45 a.m, and it is still very dark outside. The streetlights buzz by in a dizzying array as Michael speeds up to the Bold Advertising Building and hurries into the underground garage parking area for the company. He enters the elevator, taking him from the underground garage up to the main floor of the building, and then transfers to the main suite of elevators going down into the mailroom. He is not detected by the security guard, watching SportsCenter on his phone. Michael is visibly frazzled as he walks into the mailroom, but surprisingly, Buns is there, and he is sorting mail.

"Buns!," Michael says.

"Yo' Mike, where you been? I b..b..been lookin and waiting for you," Buns explains.

Michael is frantic.

"Look, man, I'm sorry for the way I've treated you lately, but I really need your help now…"

Buns sees the terror in Michael's eyes, and his heart is softened.

"I got you, man. Talk to me," Buns assures.

"A lot of bugged-out shit is happening to me… That freak Scratch… he opens doors… and when he does… bad things come through… I didn't remember him at first, but then it came to me, I've been seeing him in all of those nightmares I was telling you about that I was having… I was seeing him in my dreams before I ever actually met him, man, how is that possible?" Michael asks.

"Are you sure?" Buns asks.

"Yeah, I'm sure!" Michael says.

"Oh man…okay…that's bad…that's really bad… That means he m…m… marked you…," Buns confesses.

"What does that mean?" mark?" Michael asks.

"It means, that you were chosen or pre-selected as a victim or target of dark magic. He wanted to d…draw you closer towards him. So, he's been watching you all along, and was able to enter your dreams, to warp your reality and draw you to him…," Buns says.

"Well, it worked! All that voodoo shit is real… I wished for Betancourt to stop bothering, and it worked for a while. But that fucking wish box did more than just control Betancourt. It also gave me money, women, the promotion, and all that… even though I didn't actually ask for those things…," Michael states, almost near tears.

"The thing is, in exchange for all of that – there's a cost – and the cost is my soul. In order to maintain the material things that I received. The box makes me do things man…sick shit… I'm cursed, bro. The box turns me into a demon, a monster, and I am forced to eat human flesh…," Michael confesses.

"Yeah… I umm… know…," Buns replies softly and looks away.

"Wait, hold up, what the fuck is going on here? How do you know?" Michael says, beginning to become noticeably annoyed.

"Yo' how come you ain't even surprised about none of this shit I'm tellin' you?"

"Because, my uncle told me…," Buns says.

"Your uncle told you about some bad shit that was happening to me, and you didn't bother or think to fucking share that information with me, or try to help me?" Michael says.

"I just f…f..found out about it, and I was looking for you, to tell you and explain. Look, there's still a chance we can reverse this shit, but I n…n…need you to start from the beginning and tell me everything leading up to you getting the box, no matter how small of an issue you may think it is," Buns states.

Michael is furious at Buns. But, recognizing he has nowhere else to go, he pauses and starts talking, with his teeth clenched the whole time.

"…So, what I didn't tell you… is that part of the reason, Betancourt is bullying me… Part of the reason, is because I saw him screwing Mr. Freeman's daughter, Tiffany… He saw me looking, and he wanted to keep me in check to make sure that it would never get back to Mr. Freeman. But someone sent photocopies of him and Tiffany having sex to Mr. Freeman, which got him fired – but I swear, it wasn't me," Michael says.

"So, why didn't you tell me that from the beginning? Yo, so was any of that shit that you told me about Betancourt bullying you actually real?" Buns asks.

"Yes, it was! That was the whole reason I agreed to go see Scratch in the first place! And you have the balls, to even ask me that, when you were the one who encouraged me to go to Scratch in the first place, and got me involved in all this shit!" Michael says.

"I only did so, because you said you were being bullied!" At the time, I didn't know that Scratch was doing foul shit like this,, and things would have turned out like this! I'm just saying that it's j...j... just weird that the box seemed to provide you with precisely the things you've been constantly obsessing about even before seeing Scratch, like making money, and moving up in the company..."

"So, what the hell are you trying to say, that I somehow wanted or deserve this? So, you're trying to blame me now for what happened? Is that it? That, I somehow want to be a monster and eat people? That, I wanted my soul to be taken, and my life ruined, just because I happen to be ambitious?" Michael states.

"I'm not s...s...saying that... none of this is your fault. I'm just saying that the only way we are going to undo this shit is to talk it through, to understand what happened. It's just that the lines are blurry, that's all. Like, how did the box connect... to... your ambitions, if you went there only to talk to him about stopping the bullying?" Buns probes.

Michael pauses a minute.

"Scratch said something like, *"The box will grant your deepest innermost wishes and dreams, spoken and unspoken…,"* Michael recalls.

"That's it! That's how he did it… He c… covered everything in his binding spell by l…l.. linking the box to what you actually asked for, but more importantly, *also, to those wishes that you didn't mention.* The box directly keyed into your inner desire for money, and obsession with changing your social status. This was to make sure that you would completely do what is required to maintain those wishes most important to you. So, when you got the b..b..box from Scratch, what were the rules he told you about using it?" Buns deduces.

"He told me, that I had to put something that belonged to a victim into the box as a sacrifice to the demon… he said to never open the box for more than 24 hours without placing an offering inside… and I saw the same information online about the wish box. But…," he pauses.

"But, what?" he asks.

"Well, when I first got the box, I stupidly left it on my desk, overnight. It was closed when I left it, but when I came in the next morning, the box was wide open, and there would have been no one around late night, except…," he pauses again.

"Except, what?"

"Ms. Ella… She would have been cleaning the floor overnight, and must have seen the box on my desk, and opened it… shit… She must have opened it, and it was left open without anything being offered or placed into it… When she did that, it probably broke the contract of the box, which then freed Betancourt from the spell that was cast for Betancourt," Michael speculates.

"Okay, but if that's the case, that's also the reason Ella was "marked for death" by the box. So… Mike… you, ummm… you killed Ella?" Buns asks cautiously.

He pauses, and answers reluctantly, "Yeah… but it wasn't like that… it wasn't really me… I can't control what I do; when I change, it's like, I'm in a dream, where I am aware and seeing everything happen, but it's like, I am outside my body and have no control over what I am doing. I would never intentionally hurt, Ms. Ella…"

"If Ella tampered with the box, she may have accidentally d..d..disrupted what sounds like a binding spell that Scratch cast against Betancourt, but you need to understand that's completely s…s…separate from the main curse that was put on you… Look, my uncle got a call from some people we know from the Dominican Republic, living in Orlando, and we found out that Scratch was living there, before coming here to New York. He did the exact same thing, distributing wish boxes there, like he is now doing here, now. He traffics in dark magic, and we found out that a lot of people got possessed by demons down there, because of him. He tricks people who v…v… visit him. He uses some kind of bait-and-switch strategy.

He casts the spell, and at first, it s…s…seems that his spell is working, granting them what they wanted, but then afterwards, there is a flip to that spell, and w…w…what starts out looking like the best thing ever, quickly turns to shit…What he has actually done is cursed the victim by attaching a demon to the victim's soul from the wish box. So, it starts with the victim's wishes and dreams, which appear to have been turned into gifts, which then lead to possession, transformation, and ultimately death. The victim is granted his deepest wishes, but then ultimately taken over by a demon. As the wishes come true, the victim literally becomes the exact same demon that possessed him, eventually having to eat human flesh, and in the end lose their soul – which is…exactly… what… is happening to you…," he concludes slowly, adding to the gravity of what he has just shared, and looking Michael directly in the eyes.

"This isn't just about me…I still can't fucking believe that you knew about all this shit – and didn't tell me! So, what happened to all that good magic and keeping it 100 bullshit you was preaching to me, before? Some fucking friend you are…," Michael adds coldly.

"I told you, we didn't know, what Scratch was doing, until just recently. But there's more I need to tell you… If you k…kill and eat human flesh six times, you w…w…will become permanently stuck in demon form and will never be able to change back to human again," he states.

Michael gets up in his face angrily.

"You fucking son of a… Tell me something, I don't already know! I've already killed five times! So, I'm basically, already there! You got any more fucked up shit to tell me?" Michael yells.

Michael suddenly lunges at Buns, transforming partially into demon form, forces Buns down on his knees, and, standing over him, grabs him roughly by his neck, choking him while roaring and hissing. His eyes turn black, and his bottom jaw dislodges, causing his mouth to open wide directly above Buns' head. Michael angles and maneuvers his mouth above Buns' head like a giant cobra about to swallow a large ostrich egg. Buns' entire head is now deep within Michael's mouth. The quasi-demon's breath is hot and rancid. It begins salivating excessively as copious amounts of spit start dripping from the razor-sharp fangs and falling onto Buns' head. As he transforms, the demon within him rejoices again, as it now prepares to consume this prized final meal – providing the demon with the permanent earthbound status it so desperately covets with this kill. But Buns doesn't fight back and offers little resistance as he prepares for certain death, with only apologetic tears streaming down his face. However, preparing to face his end, he summons the courage to speak.

"Mike, I'm sorry! I'm so sorry, man! I know this is some fucked up shit, and I may deserve to die, but listen to me, don't let the demon win! Don't let it take your soul! The demon is driving you closer to kill six times, but if you do that, there's no coming back bro… the demon will try to force that to happen, but you have to fight it, and I can help you... I'm not going to let you deal with this alone! I'm going to fix this and make it right!" Buns says.

The demon's gigantic maw is poised to fit Buns' entire head into its mouth and decapitate him. However, just when it appears that the demon will completely bite Buns' head off, suddenly the demon stops, as something within Buns' words touches Michael's soul – and he withdraws and lets Buns go. After a moment, the flash of anger passes, and Michael returns to human form and releases Buns, who is still gagging from being throttled, and eyes now wide with fear, based on how close he came to dying.

They both fail to notice that Dirk has snuck into a far corner of the room from a rear exit, witnessed the entire conversation, and is both overwhelmed and intrigued by what he has just seen.

"Look, I know you don't really care about this, but you're not the only one going through this…. Scratch has trapped and t…t… tricked a lot of other people… He serves an evil and cannibalistic voodoo deity called Congo Savanne. Through the Book of the Dead, he somehow merged voodoo practices with Satanism, creating a new and incredibly powerful demonic force. His goal is to turn people on earth into demons, and recreate hell on earth… Uncle Philbert told me that h…h…he and his friend Archie, both have wish boxes… but no one has seen or heard from Archie in d..d..days, at first they thought he was alright, but now my uncle definitely feels that something bad happened to Archie, and that Scratch has something to do with it," Buns says.

"So, they are both like me? They have wish boxes, so, your uncle knew all along what would happen to me by going to Scratch? But you also said that there are a lot of other people like me who got tricked, so what happened to them…," Michael asks.

But before Buns can answer, Mr. Blake comes outside of his office.

"What the hell is all of this noise and commotion going on out here!" demands Blake.

Michael and Buns quickly exit the room and enter the elevator lobby bank. Michael frantically presses the button for the elevator. Buns turns to him to speak.

"Mike, look I'm really sorry… I…," Buns offers.

"You're sorry! You're fucking, sorry! You and your damned uncle have ruined my life! I'm cursed! Rotting from the inside, with black ooze coming out of every hole in my body! Every couple of days, I turn into a demon, eat people, and have a high likelihood of being trapped as a demon forever! So, how am I supposed to feel about all that? And all you can tell me is you're sorry… Well, that shit ain't making it man! Keep your weak ass apology, and stay the fuck away from me!" Michael states angrily.

"Look, I get that you're mad, and you have a right to be. But we have to t…t…try to get past this, and remove the curse, while there's still time! I'm sorry for taking you to Brooklyn to meet Scratch. I'm sorry about my uncle not telling us what would happen. I honestly don't know why he did that… But, I take full blame for all this – this is on me…," he says.

"You damned right, this is on you!," Michael interjects.

"…Look, I learned about this gifting thing as the only way to undo the curse, which is basically t…t… transferring the curse to someone else," Buns says.

"I already know about that," Michael says sarcastically.

"Okay… okay, well, then it sounds to me l…l… like we have the information w…w… we need to fix this," Buns offers.

The elevator arrives, and Michael goes inside, glaring intensely at Buns as the door closes, taking him up. Buns is left looking at the mirrored surface of the elevator as the door closes, but he notices that his image appears distorted. Betancourt sneaks up behind him violently, grabs him in a headlock, and places a shotgun to his head.

"Well, hello there, "ghettofabulous…" That wa…wa…was quite a moving speech y…y… You gave there. Ain't you h…h… happy to see me?" Dirk says as he mocks Buns' speech impediment. S…s…s so, I didn't hear everything, but I heard enough," Dirk states.

"See, I knew there had to be something fishy going on, with all of the sudden success that your pal is suddenly having…. So, you know what, you're going to take me to see your friend that helped Michael, and on the way, you'll fill me in, on how I can get some of that old-fashioned Black magic," Dirk says.

Dirk pulls out the saber-tooth vial of cocaine from the chain around his neck and takes a hit. At gunpoint, he forces Buns out of a side exit and into his car, which is parked behind the loading dock. He gets in the passenger seat and tells Buns to drive.

17 THE UNDERWORLD

The New York underground, including its expansive subway and sewer systems, represents a vast and cavernous underworld beneath the bustling NYC streets above.

The subway system encompasses a mix of subway stations in current use and a number of closed subway stations, which are a part of abandoned and demolished lines that were once operated by the IRT and the BMT, both privately held companies. Some subway stations are entirely abandoned and rotting away, sometimes seen by passing trains, while others are used by the transit authority as storage facilities. The sewers were built to be separate from the subway tunnels, but in many cases, the sewers run directly underneath or adjacent to the subway tunnels, making accessibility to either system from the other relatively easy. The folklore surrounding the sewers has reported that marijuana, hurriedly flushed down toilets to keep it from police and prying parents, has taken root in the sewers; fed by nutrient-rich sewage but deprived of sunlight, it has mutated into a highly potent albino form known as New York White, which is said to be extremely expensive, even for the wealthy elite who can afford it.

It is within the dark subterranean sewer connections located beneath one of the abandoned Manhattan train stations that cursed owners of wish boxes who have completed the transformation cycle, and have killed, eaten human flesh six times, and have now been permanently transformed into demons, has come to live in a colony of the damned within the sewers. It is an entire lair and underworld of monsters thriving right below the unsuspecting feet of the millions of New Yorkers who reside above. At this time, some 100 demons occupy the colony. Their very existence and grouping together fulfill what the lead demon Congo Savanne wants: to literally recreate hell on earth. The demons have all not only found each other but have bonded together and function completely like an organized pack that one would see in the wild.

The dark cavernous sewers are ideal as they are similar to the bottomless hell pit they spawned from. These supernatural beings were all once human, but because of their individual wish boxes, they have been permanently changed into ancient demons thousands of years old. Moreover, because the demons have crossed over from their metaphysical realm in hell and now occupy a physical plane on earth, they can now do the unthinkable – to procreate… A female demon in the corner of the cavern is tending to the feeding of her youngling, which she has recently given birth to. The youngling presses its snout against the mother's chin, and nudges the female's jaw, stimulating the female demon's urge, to feed its offspring.

Instinctively, she begins regurgitating contents deep within her stomach to feed her offspring. Her lower jaw disconnects from her upper jaw, causing her mouth to open to freakish proportions. The young demon then sticks its snout deep into its mother's mouth. The mother then regurgitates chunks of human flesh into the young demon's mouth, which it quickly gobbles and swallows. However, some of the contents of the nutrients she provides, fall out of her mouth onto the floor, including body parts of humans the demon has hunted, and killed for food. As an apex predator, the demons hunt unsuspecting humans, for food. Generally, preying upon those unfortunate souls who either stumble by accident into the lair of the demons or are targeted and hunted by the demons. As a result, over time, many of the homeless population within NYC have begun to vanish, becoming helpless victims and prey to the hunting demons. Homeless people who sleep in the subways, seeking shelter and heat at night, especially during the winter, are watched by the demons and then attacked for food to help feed the colony. Very rarely, these disappearances are even noticed, and when they are mentioned by other homeless people to the police, the complaints are generally dismissed and not investigated. So, the collective NYC underground systems create a perfect venue for the demons to shelter, remain hidden during the day, and come out at night to hunt, all going completely unnoticed.

There is no leadership among the demons, with each demon surviving independently, except female demons who have offspring. The demons are strategic in their hunting. Once they target their prey, they relentlessly pursue it until it is subdued and dispatched by the group for food. As a result, the grounds of the sewer section they live in are wholly littered with human skulls, bones, and remains.

The sewers are also home to other myths turned real in the form of monstrous-sized albino alligators, and snakes, which were either flushed down the toilet or found their way here, have joined blood-thirty rats teeming within this underground nightmare, creating this forbidden demonic underground ecosystem. This hidden sanctum of demons and the manifestation of hell on earth has been building over time. Instinctively, the demons are all awaiting the coming from the hell of their leader and alpha, Congo Savanne. The lead demon's presence on this earth will help increase their numbers and hasten the goal of turning the earth into hell. As they await the coming of their dark lord, they spend their time feeding, fighting, and breeding, dwelling in filth, chaos, and madness. As the trains run by this area 24 hours a day, it causes a rumbling and shaking of the demons' lair, which they have become used to. The masses living above have no idea of the thriving predatory world breeding below.

18 RE-GIFTING

Dirk has been gradually experiencing a psychotic departure from reality, exacerbated by his excessive drug use. As a result, he has become irrational, unpredictable, and aggressive. Dirk is holding Buns' arm behind his back, and also has the gun shoved in his back, as they walk into Scratch's building and go down the stairs into the basement.

"Well, come on now, lead me to the promised land," Dirk tells Buns.

Buns and Dirk walk down the hallway, arriving at Scratch's door, and Buns knocks. Scratch comes to the door armed with a machete, but as he opens the door slightly, Dirk sticks the shotgun through the space and points it directly at Scratch's face, and forces his way inside, as Scratch has no choice but to open the door. Dirk pushes Buns in first, and steps in behind him.

"Mr. Scratch, is it? My name is Betancourt. May I come in?" Continuing to push his way in. "Whoa, what happened to your face?" he asks sarcastically, referring to the swelling, and bruises on Scratch's face as a result of Michael's visit. However, Scratch does not respond.

"Looks like you had another gentleman caller tonight, hmmm? Anyone I know? So, my friend Buns here, was telling me on our ride down, all about the fantastic magical services you provide… Certain services that can bring wealth and power?" Dirk asserts.

Scratch looks at Buns directly with complete disbelief.

"Are you crazy! Dis' is the enemy of the boy you brought here earlier… And you have the nerve to bring this man here?" Scratch says.

"I had no choice, man…," Buns says, pointing to the shotgun in Betancourt's hand.

Scratch turning his gaze to Betancourt and saying defiantly.

"I cannot help you… You are already dead and cursed," Scratch utters.

Betancourt angrily grabs Scratch by the throat and puts the gun up under his chin.

"Now, see about that, are you so confident that if I pull this trigger, and blow your brains out, that your so-called magic will be able to save you? Hmm…, or do the law of physics not apply to you?" Dirk shoves the barrel of the gun hard against Scratch's throat causing him to gag. It seems like you and the Get Fresh Crew here, have been running some kind of voodoo half-court on me…. I knew something wasn't right. I didn't feel like myself, and come to find out it's because, you guys were buggering around behind my scenes, am I right? So, here's what we're going to do. First, you're going to tell me everything you did to me and how. Then, you're going to undo whatever hocus-pocus you did to me before… and then you're going to hook me up with my very own sparkly, wish box, and you're going to provide me with the Fast Pass version of what you gave Mikey. I heard that you're in the business of granting dreams and wishes. So, do you know what I wish for? I wish for wealth, power, and influence, but most of all – I wish for vengeance!" Dirk concludes.

Scratch is pushed up against the wall and continues to choke, from the gun barrel literally cutting off his windpipe. He feels himself beginning to blackout, and finally nods his head in reluctant agreement… As Dirk sports a wide grin on his face.

The New York City skyline is one of the most beautiful and memorable in the world. At night with its sparkling lights its breath-taking and especially spectacular, but even during the day it's completely majestic, particularly viewing it from high above in one of the city's towering office buildings, such as the view from Bold Advertising building.

Michael is deep in thought and staring out of his corner office window overlooking the city, when he hears another knock at the door.

"So, you don't call folks, anymore?," Susan purrs.

"Well, that depends on which folks we're talking about," Michael counters.

"Me… you don't call me anymore… Remember me? I hardly see you, just in the meetings, and even then, you seem so distant… You're always locked up here in the office, or at home I guess, I don't know what you do with your time. I thought we had something special," she says.

"We do… we do… I want that, believe me, I want that. It's just that I've got a lot on my mind right now and have been really busy, that's all. I am under a ton of pressure right now to perform with this new account," Michael says.

"Well, I can help ease some of that pressure…," gently rubbing his crotch.

"Look, I promise I'll give you a call when I have a free moment," Michael says while pulling himself away from her touch.

"See, there you go, again. Pushing me away. Michael, I really care about you… But you honestly seem so different, since getting your promotion… I mean, look at yourself. You look like shit, you're so pale with these dark rings around your eyes, and you always seem so angry, and your office always has these weird odors… Michael, what is going on with you? The staff are so afraid to even speak to you, because you've become verbally abusive and hostile. I remember you once told me, that if you were ever in charge, you would never behave like Dirk, or treat people the way he does – and now you dress like, look like him, and are acting just like him…," she states.

"Oh, come on! That's ridiculous! I am nothing like that asshole. Look, I'm fine. Everything is fine. I'm just under a lot of pressure right now. I have to finish this proposal I'm working on, and I'm behind," he says.

"Okay, okay…she concedes. "But I want you to know that I care about you, and I'm here for you. Please don't shut me out," she says.

"Look, I won't, I promise," Michael says.

He gives her a quick peck on the lips and then ushers her out of the office and closes the door. Maria looks up at him from her desk, and looks away…

Meanwhile, elsewhere within the Bold Advertising building, the investigators are still looking at the big screen monitors reviewing the security footage.

"Wait…wait… what's that… what's that… Slow it down… Can you pan the camera over?" Rizzo asks.

On screen, they see a maintenance closet where two employees are sneaking into and out of, obviously having a romantic rendezvous.

"What floor is this?" Rizzo asks.

"This is on the 31st Floor", Charleswell replies.

"Damn… is literally everybody in your company… fucking… This is about the fifth "romantic interlude" with employees getting it on here at your offices within just the last couple of days… What are you guys putting in the water?" Rizzo directs his question to Charleswell.

Charleswell seems bothered by the statement, and even more bothered that he has to answer on behalf of employees engaging in this behavior.

"Look, fraternization in the workplace is against our policy, but the truth is, many marriages and relationships actually start on the job… There's not much we can do to stop that – it happens…," Charleswell quips.

"All I'm saying is that I definitely need to change employers… So, aside from all of the hoochee-coochie going on here, at Pornhub, it seems like the 15th floor where the murder actually happened, was clean otherwise, with no other significant actions happening, but we need to keep looking… go to the 32nd floor, start scanning. The scan goes back clean for several days until it comes to Tiffany and Dirk in the copy room… Isn't that the owner's daughter?" Rizzo asks.

"Yes…," Charleswell states, not wanting to add any more information.

"Nice!!! On top of the copy machine - now that's real class… and from the looks of both of them they are both completely zooted out of their minds. Well, that's going to be an interesting report to have to make to him," Rizzo states.

"He knows about it, already," Charleswell mumbles.

"What! You're saying the father knows about this? So, who's that with her?" Rizzo demands.

Just then, detective Soto walks in, as Charleswell is explaining.

"His name is Dirk Betancourt, he is…or was…a senior VP here at the company, but someone sent some color Xerox copies of Dirk getting it on with the Mr. Freeman's daughter to Mr. Freeman," Charleswell says.

"Okay, so now we're getting somewhere. So, what happened when Freeman saw the pictures?" Soto asks.

"He fired him but allowed him to continue working just to hand over the work on all of his accounts and finish out the month," Charleswell states.

Rizzo starts getting excited, "Okay, so he's banging daddy's little angel, gets caught, and got fired, resulting in the loss of his comfortable life, which could make someone very angry… Sounds like a plausible trigger event to me…," Rizzo says.

"So, he's angry… but does that mean he's eating people for kicks?" Charleswell counters.

Soto jumps in, "So, about that, I got back the forensic results on the bite marks on the cleaning lady, but the results were inconclusive, the report showed signs of both human and some unknown form of DNA… They ran the report again and this time the results came back as unknown… So, the sample must have gotten contaminated somehow… However, we did have much better luck on the search of all of the employees on the 32nd, 31st, 15th and basement levels, and we just cross-checked that against the home addresses of all Bold Advertising employees, living within a 1 mile radius of where that copycat homicide in Brooklyn took place, as well as the subway killings, and the alley behind the building, where we found the missing cops body from the subway attack, which coincidentally was the exact same building where the double homicide of the two girls happened, and from all of that – we got exactly one match…"

He pulls out the mug shot of Michael.

"One, Michael Hill…," he says.

Just then, on one of the monitor screens, shows footage from one of the other cameras on the floor, and on that fateful night shows Michael watching Dirk and Tiffany intently from the shadows, and then running away.

"Well, speak of the devil! There's our boy on the big screen right now, watching the whole love fest with the boss' daughter…," Rizzo says.

"Look, with all due respect, just because he may have witnessed them having sex, and coincidentally happens to live within a radius of the murders, but what does that prove? That's all circumstantial and doesn't prove anything. He's not your killer… He's a valued part of this company, they just gave him a seventy-five-thousand-dollar Gold

Rolex as a gift because they value him as an asset, for Pete's sake…," Charleswell states.

Rizzo completely ignores what Charleswell is saying and speaks directly to Soto.

"Any priors?" Rizzo asks.

"Some small-time stuff as juvies for possession back in the day… Got arrested with one Egbert Thomas AKA "Buns…" Now, this guy's record and criminal history is a bit more substantial and interesting, and it turns out that he's an employee here at Disneyworld also. Do you know this guy?" Soto states.

He pulls out a mugshot of Buns, which shows his visible single gold tooth upper row, right side of his mouth.

"Yes, he works in the mailroom, which is… where Michael Hill also used to work, before he got promoted…," Charleswell reluctantly adds, as he knows how it will be viewed by the officers.

"Wow, now this is getting interesting! This could be our guy… So, even with a record, these two still got hired for fancy jobs in a place like this?" Rizzo asks.

Charleswell does not want to answer any more questions, as he feels like he is implicating all of his friends at the company. "… Yeah, the manager of the mailroom… he served some time himself… So, he decided to pay it forward and give both boys a chance…that's how they started here," Charleswell hangs his head down and looks the other way.

"We got a real-life Cinderella story here… So, let me get this straight, this Michael Hill started in the mailroom, and then somehow got promoted to the big time. Became a real big-shot, ad exec, here at the company. Says here, promoted to company VP, with all the trimmings. Real rags-to-riches shit… Hey Rizzo, check the employee headcount list the night of the murder here, and see if our friend Michael Hill was here?" he says.

"Yes, the building's security ID systems show him here all night… Except…"

"Except what?" he asks.

"Except when we had the building on lockdown and did a search on each floor, he was not physically accounted for," Rizzo says.

"Means he was here, but got out somehow," Soto adds.

"So, come on man, what are you suggesting that Michael literally ate Ms. Ella, and the people in the subway, like some kind of whacked-out Jeffery Dahmer?" Charleswell asks angrily.

"Seems crazy right? You know, I don't know the answer to that yet… But, I don't question what the evidence shows me… I just move forward assuming anything and everything is possible based on the evidence, until I'm shown otherwise – so I want to speak to Betancourt as well, but for right now this guy is definitely a person of interest. Where is Hill, right now?" Soto clarifies.

Charleswell runs a check of the security system, frantically clicking on the mainframe's keyboard.

"Hill is here, his ID badge status says, he's actually upstairs right now, on the 32nd floor, and Betancourt's ID badge just checked in on the 32nd Floor as well.", Charleswell confirms.

"Gentlemen, let's roll! Rizzo, call for back-up! Let's go!" Soto barks.

They all pull out their guns and run to the elevators.

Michael is sitting at his desk, and he feels the metamorphosis starting to change him again. His cell phone rings. It's Tiffany, she's frantically upset.

"Michael help me! It's Dirk, he's gone crazy...," she yells into the phone.

"Tiffany, where are you?" Michael asks. She replies frantically, "He brought me up to the 33rd Floor, I tried to fight him... I was able to get away and call you... You have to come up upstairs, now... Michael, please hurry..." The phone call abruptly ends.

Michael grabs the black duffle bag that he now carries the wish box in for security purposes. He takes off his Rolex and throws it in the bag, along with a few other personal items. He feels himself getting hungry for flesh but resists the metamorphosis and rushes out of his office and takes the stairs one flight up to the 33rd floor. The floor is dark and cold, except for the portable construction lights.

"Tiffany!" he calls.

No response. It is so cold that Michael sees his breath as he calls for Tiffany. He continues frantically walking across the floor looking for her amidst all the construction equipment and building materials.

"Tiffany!" he calls a second time.

Finally, he hears giggling. And sees the silhouette of a naked girl behind a white drop cloth a few feet away.

"What took you so long, baby…," Tiffany coos.

Michael goes behind the drop cloth hanging on a line. The drop cloth is separated into two sections, one that Tiffany is in and the other that Michael is in. There is a construction light on a tripod which is turned on and illuminates both of their sections, casting a shadow outline of both of them on the drop cloth. Tiffany is completely naked.

"Tiffany, what are you doing? Where is Betancourt?" he asks.

"Ummm… he's not here…," she says as she begins giggling.

"What are you talking about?" he demands.

"I made it all up…so that I could get you up here – alone…," she confesses.

Michael shakes his head. As she comes close to his section, the only thing separating them is the series of construction drop cloths that are hanging from wiring running across the room. The construction lights, which are on, display the alluring silhouette curves of her body.

"Why did you do this? Where are your clothes? It's freezing up here," he states.

"I told you I would get you, one way or the other...," she says coyly.

Michael drops his duffle bag to the ground. Still behind the drop cloths, and not completely visible to Tiffany, Michael begins to slowly morph, his turn black, his hand changes into demon form. The demon within is hungry, but also violently warping Michael's mind, and causing him to become more violent and evil. He picks up a nearby pipe at first, seemingly to potentially bludgeon her with it, in his partially transformed state. He begins to transform further and through the drop cloth it is noticeable that he is holding the pipe, but as he further transforms and tears off his clothes he hunches over and is also now naked and morphs into full monster form. The demon's burning red eyes are lustfully fixed on the young girl. The demon becomes aroused at the prospect of the naked girl nearby, revealing its massive, in-human male appendage far exceeding the dimensions in both girth and length of the pipe in its hand, which it now drops.

"Michael, don't you want me?"

She turns her back away from him at this point, so she is not seeing him changing just a few feet away…

"I mean, what does a girl have to do, to get you to…"

She turns around and now sees Michael, completely in demon form, and screams in panic, and begins to turn and run away from Michael. Just then, Betancourt steps through the exit door, which is behind them, and is holding a wish box under his arm along with the gun, and a machete he took from Scratch, tucked in his belt. Both Buns and Susan are with him, and both of their hands are tied, as Betancourt pulls them into the room. The demon's passions quickly subside, as it now faces a threat to its territory, and intended prey.

"I went to look for you in your office, and had a hunch that you would want to have more privacy up here on the unfinished floor, but I had no idea that you were having a party…" says Betancourt.

Betancourt takes a hit from the cocaine vial, and seeing Tiffany running away, morphs his hand into demon form and picks up a 2x4 and hurls it like a javelin at her from across the room with superhuman strength, and it goes straight through her chest leaving a large gaping hole, killing her. She falls to the ground with a thud. Betancourt's eyes flash black, confirming his possession, and then revert back to human.

"I guess it never ends, huh? So, now you're even trying to take my sidepiece from me… I mean, when will you finally stop trying to be me, Michael?" Betancourt yells angrily.

Michael now in full demon form roars and growls at Betancourt and attempts to take a step forward…

"Now… Now… Let's not be too hasty," he states and points the shotgun at both Buns and Susan, who now come into view.

"Look, who else I brought to the party, bud, your boy, "Bunzie!" We just came from Brooklyn, seeing our other good friend Mr. Scratch, by the way, he'd like to express his regards…," Dirk proclaims.

Betancourt is also carrying a satchel and he throws it down on the ground, and out slides the Book of the Dead along with Scratch's severed head. His eyes have been gouged out, presumably to neutralize his incantations, but he has also been shot in the head. It is clear that even though Scratch was formidable, he succumbed to a far stronger, and more ruthless predator in the form of Dirk.

"Whoops… looks like ole' Scratch completely lost his head over all this… He laughs hysterically. Hey Mikey, on the way up, look, who me and "Bunzie" ran into – it's Susie… Sweet Susie… Say hello Suzie…," Dirk says.

Michael in demon form, ignores Scratch's head on the floor and focuses intently on Dirk. However, he also recognizes Buns and Susan, and temporarily stands down. Buns and Susan both have their hands bound with duct tape. Michael in demon form, growls and steps forth to lunge at Betancourt.

"Now, you wouldn't want me to hurt this delicious little ghetto flower, would ya?" He grabs Susan and points the gun at her head.

Betancourt then, while still holding the gun, re-adjusts his grasp on Susan, his eyes turn black, he opens his mouth, and extends an exaggerated and freakishly long and serpent-like forked tongue, out of his mouth, and licks the complete side of Susan's face and head, leaving a sticky trail of black saliva and mucous bits on her face and hair…

"Mmmmm…. Chocolate, my favorite…," he says in a completely deranged sounding voice.

Susan, completely repulsed, screams, and strikes him in the face scratching his check with her nails. He violently grabs her, throws her to the ground, pinning her hands down, and gets on top of her leaning over her face. He viciously rips and tears her blouse partially open.

"You snotty little black bitch! You always thought you were too good for me, right? Well, you won't feel that way after we share some bodily fluids… Why honey? you're shivering, are you cold? You'll feel much better once I put something hot inside you! So here, let me help you with that…," he says.

Betancourt forces Susan's mouth open, then opens his mouth and projectile vomits hot black ooze with steam coming from it, directly into her mouth. She swallows some, gags, and chokes, spitting the rest out. It leaves a black oily residue containing maggots on her face. Wiping his mouth from the vomit bits remaining on his lips.

"See, now doesn't that feel better?" he asks.

Michael, in demon form, again attempts to rush Betancourt. But Betancourt re-aims the gun at Susan's head, causing Michael to stop.

"Mikey, Mikey, Mikey… You know, you really have caused me a lot of trouble… At the same time, I also have to thank you – because with the power I now have, thanks to you – I am completely free! I mean, being a demon is liberating! You understand, don't you? With this power, there are no limits to what we can do. This is better than sex, drugs, cars, money, or any of that fake superficial shit people worship man – this is real!" Dirk proclaims. His voice now becoming more distorted as he continues.

"Corporate culture is a microcosm of the real world. The corporate world has its own unique ecosystem of hunters and prey because in any office environment, you have the strong and the weak. The strong kill and eat the weak! Only the strongest will rise to the top. With this power, we are the ultimate apex predator! So, we can do more than just rise to the top – we can completely take it over! So, guess what, old man Freeman is history, as the former head of Bold Advertising. Moving forward, I will be taking control of the company! Hell, it's no wonder you chose magic as your path to get ahead and have it all! If I had known about all this power – I would have sold my soul years ago!" Dirk emphatically proclaims.

"But, unfortunately for you, there can't be two apex predators within the same ecosystem… You and I have some unfinished business…

You know, before Scratch died screaming and begging, he told me that you stole my fucking comb, and burned my hair to turn me crazy, you fucking piece of shit! You took my job…my money…my woman… Dirk's eyes are now transitioning from black to burning red. You messed around with my life and took everything from me! You literally tried to become me… I spent so many nights wondering how all of this good fortune seemed to be going your way. While so much misfortune seemed to be coming to me… And come to find out, just like a dirty little cheat, you were using black magic to rig everything in your favor. So, before your ole' buddy Scratch said his final and painful farewell, he gave me the express voodoo upgrade – So that we could level the playing field a bit," Dirk concludes.

He holds up his hand, and in the palm, we notice there is a fresh black-colored wound in his palm, and his voice becomes even coarser, and demonic…

"So, I've got my own wish box, and made my own wishes…and I've got so much to show you… you have no idea… I'm going to take back from you, every damn thing that you took from me!" he yells.

Betancourt throws down his wish box on the floor and immediately starts to rapidly morph into a demon. The construction lights begin flickering and Betancourt begins to transform. However, Betancourt's demon form is different from Michael's in that he is black with a reddish hue, but otherwise identical. He roars and picks up one of the mobile construction lights and throws it at Michael. The light stand hits Michael in the head, knocking him down, but when the light lands, it sparks a fire which begins spreading across the floor. The two demons circle each other snarling and growling and begin savagely attacking each other. Dirk attacks using his elongated claw to skewer Michael in the shoulder. Michael counters by using his elongated claw to repeatedly shank Dirk in the stomach, ripping out some of his intestines. Michael grabs Dirk's arm, and breaks it, with the bone showing through the skin. He screams in pain, but immediately it begins to heal, and he snaps the arm back into place. The demons continue savagely biting, scratching, and punching each other. They run vertically up the walls and to the ceiling and are fighting upside down suspended from the ceiling.

Michael has an advantage because he is more experienced in being in demonic form than Dirk. However, Dirk is determined, and sucker punches Michael's demon, temporarily stunning him. Michael scratches Dirk in the face, literally tearing his head and face open. However, instantly the wounds begin to heal, and he recovers sucker punching Michael, and grabbing him by the neck. Buns frees himself from the duct tape, grabs the gun, and fires several rounds into Betancourt's back. This angers him, and he lets go of Michael, and lunges after Buns, scratching his shoulder, severely wounding him. Susan screams! Michael jumps on top of Betancourt, biting him savagely and following up with several violent slashes with his claws. Betancourt counters with a punch to Michael's wounded shoulder, and then tries to bite Michael in the face. Michael grabs Betancourt's head with his two hands and literally tries to pull his head off, but as he pulls, Betancourt's neck heals as it stretches to freakishly long dimensions extending along with his head and not allowing for decapitation. Betancourt punches Michael in the throat, which forces him to let go of Betancourt. Betancourt is now a bit unbalanced, with his head now disjointedly dangling from an overly elongated neck. His head darts about like a serpent as it heals and begins to retract into place. However, as Betancourt's head returns to its normal position, Michael again grabs for his head, but this time Betancourt attempts to bite his hands. Michael seizes this opportunity and grabs both his upper and lower jaw, and begins to force them apart, eventually snapping, and breaking Dirk's bottom jaw. The demon howls in pain, with its jaws separated and broken, but again begins immediately healing. Buns is mortally wounded, with the blood spurting out of his shoulder, he crawls over to the box that Betancourt dropped. He picks it up.

"Hey Betancourt… over here… Hey asshole… look over here…," Buns says.

Betancourt in demon form turns around to look. Buns picks up Betancourt's wish box.

"On your behalf, Dirk Betancourt, I am hereby gifting your wish box to me, which I freely accept of my own free will, and accord… Thank you Dirk, for your gift!" Buns proclaims.

Buns presses his palm down on the spike, there is a loud cracking sound, and the demon that was previously in Betancourt now vacates Betancourt, exiting from his mouth as a black plume of ectoplasm with a face, and flies above Buns circling and angrily wailing, before finally entering into Buns. Betancourt then reverts to quasi-human form, and Michael swiftly decapitates him, with a clawed swipe to the neck. Red blood spurts from his neck, and his arms are still moving around and fighting. Finally, his body drops to his knees, with his arms still swinging and flailing about, eventually falling to the floor with a thud. At the same time, Buns' eyes are now black, indicative of demonic possession, and he begins to morph into a demon. He gets up and limps over to Michael's wish box which is on the floor, in the corner. He picks it up, and presses his palm down on the spike, looking directly at Michael. He is trembling, and his voice sounds coarse and demonic.

"On y…y… your behalf, Michael Hill, I am hereby gifting your wish box to me, which I freely accept of my own free will and accord… Thank you Michael for your gift!" Buns proclaims.

There is a loud cracking sound, and the demon inside of Michael vacates his body leaving from his mouth as a thick black plume of ectoplasm with an evil face, which angrily flies in circles, snarling above Buns' head. Buns raises his arms upwards, and provokes the demon.

"Yes, take me! Take me, dammit! "Come into me!" he yells.

The demon spirit then savagely enters into Buns through his chest. Michael now reverts to normal, and Buns' eyes are now red, and he begins to morph into a large grotesque, winged demon, with two ram horns extending from both sides of his head, and a devil's tail extending from his lower back. But as he transforms, Buns fights to resist the full transformation. He limps over to Betancourt's shotgun on the floor, with his demonic wings fluttering behind him, he kneels, picks up the shotgun, and places the stock on the floor, leans over, and places the barrel to his forehead. With his elongated claws, he has difficulty pulling the trigger. However, he finally succeeds, but the gun slides over so that bullet glances off the side of his head, only partially blowing off the side of his head… He drops to the floor, with his wings fluttering as he is still partially alive… Susan screams, and Buns' eyes revert to human… Michael rushes over to his friend and tenderly holds Buns' head up.

"I t…t..t.. told you, this was my fault. So, I… f.. fixed… it…"

"Buns! What did you do! Oh God, what did you do! You didn't have to do this! We could have found another way! I'm sorry! I'm sorry for all the things… all the bad things, I said to you! You were right about everything… about life, about money – it doesn't bring you happiness! It doesn't… I know that… I know that now… but please… please … don't die. Why… why did you do this?" Michael in desperation pleads.

"For you, Bro… I did it f…f… for you, I took the curse away…so, that you could be free… He coughs up bright red blood. "You did it Bro? You made it… to the top of the corporate ladder, and it wasn't the wish box that took you there – you did that – it was you… it was you the whole time," says Buns. His breathing is becoming more labored and difficult. "We… we… still Brothers… right?"

Michael pauses, with tears streaming down his face.

"Yo' Always…," Michael responds.

Michael sobs uncontrollably as Buns' head rolls to the side, his body goes limp, and he closes his eyes as the last bit of life ebbs out of him… Both demons that were in Buns now vacate his body, screaming and wailing, and fly back into their separate wish boxes, which are on the floor. Buns returns to human form, with an almost angelic look on his face. Michael drapes his naked body with a piece of drop cloth from the construction site.

Susan is wide-eyed and in complete shock over what she has seen. She is unsure of what to do at this point. She tries to quietly run away, but Michael sees her, and puts his hands up trying to calm and reassure her…

"No, no… it's me, it's okay… the curse is broken… you don't have to run… I'm not going to hurt you… it's okay… it's okay… I know you're scared, and you've seen some bat shit crazy shit… and I promise you, I'll explain everything… but right now, if you really care about me, I need you to trust me – please.", he pleads.

"You're safe now and I would never hurt you… But with everything that's happened, I can't stay here… The cops will be looking for me… So, I have to get out of New York, and try to start over… Look, I can't offer you the money and trappings of this corporate life anymore – but it's all an illusion and a trap anyway. But, I do love you Susan, and the one thing that I can offer you is my genuine heart and all of my love…

So, I am going to ask you again, one last time – Will you come away with me?", he asks looking lovingly into her eyes.

Fire is raging all around them, giving the floor a hellish appearance. Michael extends his hand to her. She is a bit pensive at first… But then she takes his hand, and they embrace. He kisses her on the forehead, and they begin heading towards the back stair exit. As he is leaving, he picks up his duffle bag, and puts on some shorts and a t-shirt he had in the bag. He then takes out his gold Rolex from the bag, and puts it on Buns' wrist, and then takes the grillz out of Buns' pocket and places it in directly his hand. He then takes a burning 2x4 on the ground and uses it to set Buns' body on fire, starting with the face. He then picks up his wish box but leaves Betancourt's box behind next to Buns' body… Susan props him up to help him walk, as he has been seriously injured from the recent fight. He pauses, looking into her eyes.

"I just need to make sure that this is completely over for me, and to also pay back someone partly responsible for all this… I need to stop by my office on the way out," Michael says.

Intense patches of fire rage all around them. Michael and Susan go down the back stair entrance, just as Officer Rizzo, Detective Soto, and Charleswell arrive on the floor from an additional staircase on the other side of the floor. The fire is raging throughout the floor now and has already severely burned at least one of the bodies.

"This one looks like Betancourt over here, or what's left of him… I also got a head over here, with no body…," says Soto.

"There's a naked blonde over here… Looks like the owner's daughter, with a serious hole in her chest… and another body over here which is covered by a drop cloth but is on fire!" Rizzo says.

Rizzo uses another nearby drop cloth to smother and extinguish the flames and stop the body from burning.

"It's hard to see who this is, the face and body are too badly burned, but I see what looks like a Rolex… Hey, looks like we got our perp Michael Hill over here! He has some kind of weird looking wooden-box… and wait a minute, what the fuck! Look at this, he's holding some kind of fanged mouthpiece in his hand… This must be how the sick son of a bitch chewed up the victims and ate them…," he says.

Charleswell specifically goes over and looks at the body with Rolex and looks into the mouth and sees Buns' gold tooth – so he knows that the body is not Michael and is really Buns, but he does not say anything.

"What the hell really happened here… Some kind of sick, cannibal, Jeffery Dahmer love triangle gone wrong? There are so many bodies…," Rizzo says.

Rizzo uses a pen and begins to carefully retrieve the Rolex watch and the Grillz platinum fangs, and places them in a plastic police evidence bag.

"Don't know, but whatever it was, it looks like it's over now. There's nothing more we can do, and we need to get the hell out of here before the whole damn building burns to the ground," Soto says.

"Wait… Just let me grab this weird-looking box, it may be evidence… Oh shit!!!"

He grabs the wish box, but immediately yells and drops the box, with his palm bleeding. The vengeful and angry demon within the box is wrathful because of the gifting that has taken place, so it quickly leaps out of the box and aggressively enters Officer Rizzo…he immediately falls to the ground and his eyes become briefly black, and he is in a trance-like state.

"Rizzo! What the hell! Rizzo, you okay? Charleswell, give me a hand with him. We got to get out of here!" Soto orders.

EMS workers arrive and immediately begin to rush in and assist, they quickly begin to place the dead bodies on stretchers and rush them to the staircase. Detective Soto and Mr. Charleswell place both of Rizzo's arms around their necks and help to literally drag him out to the stairs as the flames engulf everything, including the dead bodies. However, the Book of Dead, overlooked and left behind does not burn amidst the intense flames.

Fire trucks begin arriving outside the building, as flames are seen jutting out of the top floor of the building, placing obvious questions and doubts on the future of this company.

EPILOGUE

(One Year Later, In the Offices of Bold Advertising)

The damage to the building was successfully contained to just the upper 33rd floor. While there was extensive water and smoke damage to the other floors, structurally the building survived and remained intact. Jessica Reyes-Powell has been named CEO of Bold Advertising, in the wake of Roger Freeman stepping down. The board in its letter to the staff applauded Jessica for her leadership skills, which are necessary in righting the ship and leading the company forward during this dark time. Jessica has named Jimmy, Vice-President of the Account Division, and he is now moving into Michael's old office.

"So, Jimmy, you're the new office unicorn kid! Let me be the first to say, that you're beginning your Corporate Climb... Now, I don't have to tell you that the board and I are really counting on you stepping up to manage the account division, and essentially replace both Michael and Dirk... I still can't believe that there has been so much death and suffering here, Michael, Dirk, Tiffany, all gone, just like that…", she states with tears in her eyes.

"With the fire, and all of the murders, so much has happened and changed around here. I mean Freeman has completely disappeared and become a recluse, but despite all of that, somehow, we are going to keep this company going. The way I look at it, it's like we've experienced our own slice of hell and somehow come through it. But look, in the end, neither one of us made out to badly, right? She says rhetorically. You even got Michael's new mahogany desk in the deal!

"Yeah, I guess so… I just have a few personal items to unpack, but thank you Jessica, for this promotion, and for everything… I am really looking forward to this new role and working alongside you to keep this ship afloat," Jimmy says.

"Great! Glad to hear it! Well, I got a run, so I'll see you later!" she says as she closes the door behind her. Jimmy looks at the banker's box, and at the top is a bright red lipstick, and an interoffice manila envelope containing additional color Xerox copies of the tryst that Dirk and Tiffany had. He pulls the envelope open and begins looking at the Xerox images focusing on Tiffany.

"I loved you so much, and you never even took the time to notice me… So, I did what I had to do… I wish I never even met you…," he says angrily.

"Now, let's see, if Michael has left me any gifts in his desk…," he says aloud.

He begins to pull each desk drawer open. In the bottom right drawer, he sees Michael's sparkling wish box. The eyes of the demons etched into the wish box are shimmering and look like tiny specs of gold glitter. He feels and hears the wish box calling out to him. He can't resist it… There is a note on top. The note reads, *"To whom it may concern – this gift is for you!"* Jimmy smiles greedily as he takes the box out of the drawer, and tries to open it, but instead, immediately pricks his palm on the sharp top edge. His blood flows into the box, and the demon within angrily flies out of the box, and directly into his chest.

"Owww… my hand! Dammit, Mike! Some damn gift you left me… I swear you're killing me, man…You're killing me…," he says – as his eyes turn completely black, with a sudden sound of rapid, repetitive, and incomprehensible loud whispering all around him saying –

"All That Glitters Is Not Gold!"

ABOUT THE AUTHOR

Kevin Delano Hughes is an author and former adjunct college professor of Humanities. He hails from America's Paradise in the U.S. Virgin Islands – St. Thomas, USVI. As an African-American and Caribbean author, he draws upon the duality of his rich cultural heritage to fuel his intense passion for storytelling. As a dynamic new storyteller, his interest in the elevated and social horror genres has provided a fertile ground for his creative mind to develop intricate stories that will frighten, entertain, intrigue, and transport the reader into the dark world of the story, experiencing the plot as it twists and unfolds, building to an often-unexpected crescendo. Kevin's goal as a writer transcends merely providing a good old-fashioned scare, but also encompasses providing a bold, compelling, socially conscious narrative that will resonate with readers. In "Corporate Climbing", the author captures identifiable snapshots of life within a dysfunctional workplace filled with many toxic "isms": racism, elitism, sexism, classism, etc. Hughes introduces a supernatural defining event and then proceeds to blend the macabre with the modern. As a horror-thriller, the story pays homage to the horror genre as well as providing its own nuances, which the author trusts readers will enjoy, remember, and appreciate based on the use of unconventional protagonists, set within interesting situations, yielding to spine-chilling and often unexpected results.

www.ingramcontent.com/pod-product-compliance
Lightning Source LLC
Chambersburg PA
CBHW070506300726
48975CB00007B/2340

* 9 7 9 8 2 1 8 2 5 8 8 0 1 *